# "Stop!"

Skye looked around and was surprised to see that she recognized the road they were on. Now was as good a time as any to start making some new memories.

"What?" Jake asked in alarm as he slammed on the brakes.

"We used to park here, remember?" She undid her seat belt and slid over to him. "We used to stop here on the way home."

She grinned nervously at him. Yes, she wanted to get home to Grace, but she'd been in a bed—by herself—for the past four months. It was time to fix that starting right *now*.

Jake was stiff in her arms. "We did," he said through gritted teeth.

"Are you going to kiss me, Jake Holt?" she whispered against his lips.

He turned his head. "The doctor said— He said we shouldn't stress you out too much. Physically."

Skye sighed in disappointment. "Not even if I want to be stressed? Just a little? Not even a kiss?"

Jake didn't reply for a moment. Then he sort of chuckled and said, "When we used to stop here, I don't remember it ever being *just* a kiss."

# His Lost and
# Found Family

## SARAH M.
## ANDERSON

First published in Great Britain 2015
by Mills & Boon, an imprint of Harlequin (UK) Limited,
Large Print edition 2015
Eton House, 18-24 Paradise Road,
Richmond, Surrey, TW9 1SR

© 2015 Harlequin Books S.A.

Special thanks and acknowledgment are given to
Sarah M. Anderson for her contribution to the
*Texas Cattleman's Club: After the Storm* miniseries.

ISBN: 978-0-263-26030-4

Harlequin (UK) Limited's policy is to use papers that
are natural, renewable and recyclable products and made
from wood grown in sustainable forests. The logging
and manufacturing processes conform to the legal
environmental regulations of the country of origin.

Printed and bound in Great Britain
by CPI Antony Rowe, Chippenham, Wiltshire

## SARAH M. ANDERSON

Award-winning author Sarah M. Anderson may live east of the Mississippi River, but her heart lies out west on the Great Plains. With a lifelong love of horses and two history teachers for parents, she had plenty of encouragement to learn everything she could about the tribes of the Great Plains.

When she started writing, it wasn't long before her characters found themselves out in South Dakota among the Lakota Sioux. She loves to put people from two different worlds into new situations and to see how their backgrounds and cultures take them someplace they never thought they'd go.

Sarah's book *A Man of Privilege* won the 2012 RT Reviewers' Choice Award for Best Harlequin Desire. Her book *Straddling the Line* was named Best Harlequin Desire of 2013 by CataRomance, and *Mystic Cowboy* was a 2014 Booksellers' Best Award finalist in the Single Title category.

When not helping out at her son's school or walking her rescue dogs, Sarah spends her days having conversations with imaginary cowboys and American Indians, all of which is surprisingly well-tolerated by her wonderful husband. Readers can find out more about Sarah's love of cowboys and Indians at www.sarahmanderson.com

To my agent, Jill Marsal,
who saved this book and quite
possibly my career by keeping calm
and carrying on, even when I couldn't.
You've made me a better writer,
and it's a joy to work with you!

# One

Jake Holt could not believe his eyes. What on God's green earth had happened to Royal, Texas?

Yeah, he'd been gone for four years after cutting off all contact with his family and his hometown. He expected some things to have changed. But this? He drove down what had been the main commercial drag. Fast-food restaurants and big-box stores all looked like someone had run over them with a freight train. He passed the hospital, where it looked as if a whole wing was missing.

Jesus. It looked as if a bomb had gone off here. Or...

Or a tornado had blown the town to bits.

The thought made him nervous. Jake cast a withering glance at the papers in the benign-looking envelope on the passenger seat. Divorce papers. Skye had sent him divorce papers. He probably shouldn't be surprised—he hadn't spoken to her in almost ten months. He'd been out of the country, setting up an IT at a new oil site in Bahrain. He'd been busy and she'd made her feelings clear.

Part of him knew the marriage was over. They wanted different things. He wanted to be free of their families and their never-ending feud over land. He wanted to wash his hands of Royal, Texas, for good. He'd wanted to get his business, Texas Sky Technologies, off the ground, which required a lot of hard work. He'd wanted to be a success and give her everything she wanted.

Except he couldn't. Skye wanted the impossible. She hadn't been able to let go of the crazy notions she'd had about coming back home and resolving the family feud and somehow bringing the Taylors and Holts together. He didn't know why. Maybe so they could join hands and sing in perfect harmony and share a soda together.

No matter what her reasons, it wasn't going to happen. The Taylors and the Holts had been arguing, suing and occasionally shooting over the same piece of land for at least a hundred years and nothing Jake did or said was going to change that. Hell, he couldn't even get his own family to accept that he'd fallen in love with Skye Taylor. How was he supposed to convince her parents to accept him as a son-in-law?

Easier just to pick up and start over somewhere new.

Or it had been, until it all fell apart.

Still, Jake could not believe that she'd actually had him served with divorce papers. Skye had been his world for so long. They'd sacrificed everything to be together once.

The papers were dated eight months ago. Jake wasn't about to sign the damn things and mail them off. Not until he made good and sure that Skye was done with him.

Which was why he was back in his least favorite place in the entire world—Royal, Texas. If Skye could tell him to his face that it was over, then it was over. Twenty years of his life spent loving her—done.

God, he hated this town.

He'd come home after all these years on the assumption that Skye was here. But now? Now he hoped she *wasn't* here. It looked as if the tornado that had blown through town had left a wake of complete and total destruction in its path.

Despite the long months apart, and the evil divorce papers, he prayed she wasn't here, that wherever she was, she was safe. That she hadn't been in the path of that twister.

He didn't even know when the twister had hit. He was jumping to conclusions, but the whole prodigal-son-returns-home thing had him on edge. He needed information before he did anything else. And the best place to get information in this town was the Royal Diner.

As he headed into the heart of the town, the damage got worse and worse. Trees were gone, nothing but twisted stumps left. The car lot where he'd bought his first truck was vacant, save a pile of rubble where the building used to stand. Plenty of places had tarps over their roofs and boarded-up windows. The walk-up ice-cream shop where he used to take Skye for a cone was off its foundation entirely, sitting four feet away on the sidewalk where he'd dared to hold Skye's hand in public.

He'd turned his back on this town four years ago. Said he didn't care if he never saw Royal—

or the people in it—ever again. But now that he was here, it was almost too much.

Just when he thought he couldn't take it, he came upon a block that was mostly okay looking. Jake was thrilled to see the Royal Diner was still standing. People were sitting inside, drinking coffee.

He felt himself breathe. It wasn't all gone. The diner was still here.

He pulled up in front and sat, thinking. He didn't want to care about Royal, Texas, because he'd told himself for years that he *didn't* care.

But seeing the town so wounded, and not knowing who'd lived and who'd died—it tore him up in a way he wasn't prepared for. He was worried about his family, for God's sake. He was worried about Skye. Just because it was over didn't mean he hoped something awful had happened to her.

Someone walked past his car and did a double take. Jake didn't recognize the man, but then, he didn't recognize the town anymore. Things had changed.

He needed to know how *much* they'd changed. Forewarned was forearmed and he needed to know what had happened before he sucked it up and went home.

So, gritting his teeth, Jake got out of the car and walked into the diner.

What had been a pleasant midday hum died the moment the door shut behind him. He recognized Amanda working behind the counter, although he was surprised to see she was pregnant.

"Jake? Jake *Holt*?" She froze in what seemed to be true shock—or horror. "Is it really you?"

"Hi," Jake said, putting on a smile as the silence closed around him. He could feel the shock rolling off of every single person in the restaurant. Even the cook leaned out of the kitchen to look at him.

He'd been in tight spots before, dealing with angry international businessmen who didn't speak much English and had their own ways of doing things. But this? This was the tightest spot he'd ever been in.

"What?" someone demanded from one of the booths in the back of the diner. "Did someone say Jake *Holt*?"

Then, to Jake's surprise, his brother, Keaton, stood up.

"Jake?" Keaton looked at him as if Jake were a

zombie who'd stumbled into the diner fresh from the graveyard. "What the hell?"

Jake looked around the room, but he found no moral support. Everyone appeared to be thinking the same thing. Even Amanda, who'd always been a sweetheart back in school.

This was not how he'd wanted it to go. He'd wanted to locate Skye and hash it out for once and for all in *private* with no one—or at least not their families—the wiser. He wanted things to go back to the way they used to be, back when it was him and Skye against the world. And if he had to confront his family, then he'd wanted it to happen in the privacy of the Holt home, without an audience.

Which is what he had right now—one hell of an audience. The diner was mostly full with the lunch crowd. Plenty of witnesses with waggling tongues who would probably be more than happy to spread the news of the less-than-happy family reunion from here to San Antonio.

Damn.

"Hello, Keaton." Jake tried to sound as if he were glad to see his brother, but he didn't pull it off.

The diner was so quiet he could have heard a pin drop. He wasn't sure anyone was even breathing.

Keaton's jaw was clenched—and so were his fists. Yeah, this wasn't a happy family reunion by any stretch of the imagination. "Where have you been?" To his credit, at least it didn't come out as a snarl.

"Bahrain," Jake replied, trying to keep his tone casual. After all, he was basically announcing this to the whole town. "I had a big job there. It just wrapped up."

A light murmur rippled through the onlookers. Jake couldn't tell if that was a good thing or a bad thing.

"I heard about the storm," he went on. Might as well put some lipstick on this pig. "I came home as soon as I could to see if I could help."

More murmuring. At least this time, it sounded like a positive reaction.

Keaton gave him a look of white-hot death, but then he seemed to realize that they had an audience. "Do you have time to have a cup of coffee?" He motioned back to the booth.

"Sure." Just a casual cup of joe with the man

who'd forced Jake to choose between the Holt land and the woman he loved. No big deal.

He walked past his brother and slid into the opposite side of the booth. Keaton stood there, glaring down at him for a moment before he took his seat.

The diner was still unnaturally quiet—so quiet, Jake could hear Amanda's footsteps coming toward. "Coffee?"

He tried to be polite. "Sure. I take it you're not Amanda Altman anymore, huh?"

"Been married to Nathan Battle for over a year," she said with an awkward grin.

Jake nodded, hoping the gesture concealed his surprise. He'd thought they'd broken up a long time ago. "That's great. Congratulations."

"It's good you're back, Jake," Amanda said. She paused and then, after a worried glance at Keaton, added, "Things may have changed, but it's still good to come home."

He forced a polite smile. "Not sure how long I'll be here," he said. "But I'll do my best to help out."

Amanda gave him a look before the cook rang the bell and yelled, "Order up!"

And then it was him and Keaton. His brother

had changed, but then, hadn't everything? Fine lines had settled in around his eyes and his mouth. They might have been the lines that went with smiling. Maybe Keaton had been happy after Jake had slipped off into the night with Skye four years ago. Maybe he'd gotten married, had some kids. Had a nice life. Jake could be a big enough man to hope for that.

There were no smiles now.

Jake took a sip of his coffee and felt something inside him unclench. He'd had coffee the world over, but there was something about the coffee at the diner that tasted like...

Like home.

He was not going to be glad to be back, no matter what Amanda said. And he was not staying long, either. The look on Keaton's face made it plenty clear he wasn't welcome. Some things never changed.

Slowly, the noise level in the diner began to return to normal conversation levels. Still, Keaton said nothing. And Jake wasn't about to fill the void. He had *nothing* to say to his brother.

Nothing polite, anyway.

Finally, Keaton cracked. "Bahrain?"

Jake nodded. "I run a successful information technology company that specializes in creating the IT infrastructure on oil drilling sites. We do jobs around the world. The Bahrain job was a major win—I beat out some NASDAQ companies for the right to that job."

Of course, none of that information was exactly secret. If Keaton—or anyone else here in Royal—had really wanted to, they could have searched for Texas Sky Technologies online.

Keaton's jaw worked. "Texas Sky, right?"

Jake stared at him. "You looked me up?" Had his brother...missed him?

"Yeah, I really had no choice," Keaton replied with a snort. "Imagine my surprise when the people who answer your phones insisted that you didn't have a brother. Like I didn't even exist."

Okay, so Jake maybe hadn't talked about his family in warm, glowing terms with his employees, but that didn't explain why his receptionist hadn't forwarded the messages.

One other thing was clear from the way Keaton had said he didn't have a choice—the man hadn't missed Jake. "Did you ever consider it's not the rest of the world, Keaton? Maybe you just bring that out in everyone." He started to slide out of the booth. Sparring with his brother was not getting him any closer to finding Skye. He did not have time for this.

Keaton put up an arm to block Jake's exit. "How long were you there for?"

Jake was stuck. He'd come in here to get information about Skye and he still had nothing. So he gritted his teeth and settled back in. This was for Skye. "Almost ten months. It was a yearlong contract, but once you factor in the vacation time, it was just short of ten months."

"So you have no idea, then?"

"No idea about what?" Which pretty much answered the question, but that was all Jake was going to give the man.

"About Skye."

And just like that, the power balance in the booth shifted.

Jake took in the angry look on Keaton's face and did what he had to. He blurred the truth. "Bahrain isn't exactly a woman's paradise. She wasn't up to joining me on this job."

"I imagine not."

Jake didn't like his brother's sarcastic tone, and

fought the urge to lunge over the table and grab Keaton by the collar. He wasn't the same hotheaded kid. He was a businessman—a darned successful one at that. He could negotiate with businessmen from China to South Africa to Bahrain.

He would not let Keaton win. Not now, not ever.

So he let that nugget sit while he sipped his coffee. "Something you'd like to get off your chest, Keaton?" he finally asked.

"Did you at least have the decency to marry her?"

He. Would. Not. Kill. Keaton.

Not yet, anyway.

"Actually," Jake said in his coolest voice, "I don't see what that has to do with you in the least. What goes on between me and Skye is our business. Not yours." He would absolutely not tell his brother a single iota of information more than he had to—and his questionable marital status was at the top of that list.

"You should have married her." Keaton made a show of sipping his coffee.

Jake didn't want to have his brother all up in his business like this. This was not how the plan was supposed to go. He was supposed to swing into Royal, find Skye, confront her if she was here and swing right back out again. Whatever problems he and Skye had were between the two of them. Keaton was not a part this. No one in their families was.

So much for that plan.

"Again, not your concern."

"You're so sure of that, huh?" Keaton shook his head in obvious pity.

Jake bristled. Why was Keaton insisting that he should have married Skye? The man had spent years trying to push Skye and Jake apart—not enter them into holy matrimony. "Positive."

"Positive," he said, his tone deadly serious. "Oh, yeah, you're *positive*! You always did think you knew everything, didn't you?"

That was it. Jake didn't have to sit here and take this. Keaton was always doing this—lording it over Jake. Jake hadn't missed his brother at all in four years. Not once. And this was why.

"Been good seeing you, Keaton. Give my best to Mom and Dad." He tried to slide out of the booth but Keaton grabbed his shirt. Immediately, the conversation in the diner dropped to an audible whisper.

"I need to congratulate you, Jake." The sarcasm had slipped back into Keaton's tone and he had a mean glint in his eye. "You're a father."

Jake's stomach dropped. It couldn't be true. He and Skye had always been careful, always discussed waiting to start their family until they were a little better situated. No, he wasn't a father because it just wasn't possible. Instead, this was Keaton trying to screw with him, as always. He probably didn't even know where Skye was. "Funny, Keaton. Real funny." He shook free of his brother's grip and bolted out of the booth. He tried to smile at Amanda as he all but bulldozed his way out of the diner.

As he walked, his mind raced through the options. He was going to kill his brother. Keaton had always been a jerk about Jake and Skye, but this? This took the cake. Jake was not a father. Skye hadn't been pregnant when they'd called it a day.

Had she?

He thought back to the last time he'd lain in bed with her in his arms. They'd gone out to dinner—a fancy thing, because he was making more money now. Business was good. He was trying to show her that he could take care of her, give her the very best in life. But dinner had been tense. They hadn't spoken much. They'd had sex when they'd gone home, but it'd been...

It'd been missing the spark that had held them together for so long. The evening was supposed to be about showing Skye that they still had something worth saving. But apparently in the end, it'd shown them—her—that what they'd had was already gone.

A few days later, their world had erupted. Skye had insisted that, if Jake loved her, he'd go home to Royal with her and start a family. And Jake had insisted that, if Skye loved him, she never even would have asked him to come back to this pit of a town.

The fight had been—well, he tried not to think about the things he'd said. And he tried extra hard not to think about the things she'd said. He'd gone to a hotel the next morning and left for Bahrain the next week.

He could not be a *father*. He just couldn't be. And if he was—that was a huge *if*—then Skye had even less business serving him with divorce papers. But he'd had no other contact with her. Not so much as a peep.

So Jake did the only reasonable thing. He ignored his brother—who had followed him out of the diner, calling his name—and kept walking. He wasn't about to sit there and let his brother mock him. There were other ways to find Skye. Ways that did not involve additional humiliation at the hands of Keaton.

He made it to his Porsche Turbo and got the door open before Keaton caught up to him. "Wait," he repeated, shoving the door closed.

"Go to hell. You want to mock me? Fine. But I don't have to sit there and take it. For the record, I didn't come back to Royal for *you*. I didn't come back for Mom and Dad. I came back for Skye and Skye alone. We'll deal with our relationship just like we've always dealt with things—on our own. You and the Taylors and this whole town can go to hell. I'll even buy you a handbasket."

Keaton leaned against the car door so that Jake would have to go through him to open it. Which was an option that was on the table, as far as Jake was concerned. "You pigheaded fool," he started.

"That's how you want to play this? Fine." Jake's

hands curled into fists. "You're nothing but a traitor. I wouldn't trust anything you said even if you had it notarized. I tried that once, remember? I trusted you with my deepest secret and what did you do? You ran to Mom and Dad as fast as your chicken legs could carry you. You tried to break me and Skye up more times than I can count because being a Holt was more important than being with her. You are nothing to me, Keaton. We are not brothers. I am not a Holt. Not anymore."

If Keaton was insulted by this tirade, he didn't show it. Instead, he just kept on leaning against the door, looking at Jake as if he pitied him.

Jake had dreamed of calling his brother out. *Dreamed* of it. But saying those words to his face didn't leave Jake with a sense of lightness or of closure. He only felt worse. And he'd long since vowed not to feel bad about his family. Those days were over. "Get out of my way, Keaton. Or I will get you out of my way. Last warning."

"Her name is Grace."

*Grace.* He wanted to tell Keaton to go to hell again, but his voice suddenly didn't work, so he settled for glaring.

"She was eleven weeks premature," Keaton

went on. "She was in the neonatal intensive care unit for almost three months."

Images Jake had seen in movies of tiny little babies hooked up to wires and tubes suddenly overwhelmed him. He struggled to ask, "The— the hospital? Wasn't that hit during the storm?"

"She wasn't in the hospital during the storm." But damn the man, he didn't elaborate.

They stood there for a moment. Jake realized he was breathing in great gulps, but he couldn't help it.

"Aren't you even going to ask?" Keaton demanded. He sounded frustrated.

"Ask what?"

"*Anything*, man. You've had absolutely no contact with Skye in the last four months—maybe even the whole time you were being a big shot in Bahrain. You obviously have no idea what's going on."

"Maybe I do," Jake snipped, trying to keep his temper under control. He would not give Keaton the satisfaction of getting to him. He would *not*. "Maybe I've been texting with Skye this whole time. How would you know?"

"Because," Keaton replied, anger and exasperation edging his voice, "Skye's only come out of the medically induced coma the doctor's had her in a couple of weeks ago. You can't talk to a woman who's been unconscious—*oof*!"

Whatever else Keaton was going to say was crushed out of him as Jake grabbed him by the shirt and slammed him back against the car. "She *what*?"

"She's been out the last four months, Mr. Big Shot," Keaton said as he tried to push back against Jake's grip. It didn't work. "And Grace is yours. She's a Holt. All the tests came back that she was 99.9 percent positive for being a Holt, which means that her father is either me, Dad or you. And neither Dad nor I have so much as looked at Skye in four years. So it's you. She's your baby girl."

The weight of these words made Jake's knees weak. He had to step back and lean on the car's hood to keep his balance.

His baby. His and Skye's. Who'd been in a coma for months. While he'd been working in Bahrain.

Oh, God. What had he *done*?

"Where?" That was all he could get out.

"Skye's still at the hospital. She's awake, but she

doesn't remember much of anything that might have happened in the last few years. Couldn't tell us anything about where you *might* be or why."

"And…the baby? Grace?" The name felt strange on his tongue. His baby. Everything about that felt strange.

"Funny thing about her," Keaton said, after a dramatic pause that made Jake want to tear his brother apart. "She's been handed over to the closest living relatives. Which is me and Lark. You remember Skye's older sister?"

"You and…Lark?" The way Keaton had said her name—in the same sentence as his own—there hadn't been any sneer then. None of the mocking tone he'd always used when he talked about the Taylors.

"Yes. Me and Lark. We have her until Skye can take over. Or until your sorry ass showed up."

"You're taking care of Grace? *With* Lark? I thought—I thought you hated the Taylors. You hated them *so* much."

That's why he'd left. He might not care for Skye's family, but he'd loved Skye since he was seven and she was six. She'd always been more to him than a Taylor. She had been his *everything*.

Keaton looked him in the eye. "Things have changed, Jake. Welcome home."

"How are you feeling today?" The man in the white coat smiled at her.

"Better. Less…fuzzy," Skye replied. Which was the truth. She was sitting up in bed, her eyes open. Her brain was almost working. She felt as close to normal as she had since…since…

Damn. *Almost* working—but not quite.

"Do you remember my name?"

Skye thought. "You're my doctor? Dr. Wake…" She scrunched up her face as the man gave her a hopeful smile. "Dr. Wakefield? Is that right?"

"Excellent!" He nodded and made a note on the tablet he was carrying. "That's very good, Skye. Do you remember her name? She's my research assistant," he said, handing the tablet to the woman in nurse's scrubs standing next to him.

The name was there, but it kept slipping through Skye's mind like a strand of wet spaghetti. Just when she thought she had it, it slipped right past her again. "Julie? Juliet? Jules? Something like that." She leaned back against the bed. The effort of trying to remember was draining. But she didn't want to close her eyes. She was *so* tired of sleeping.

"Very good," Dr. Wakefield. "You got it on the first try—Julie Kingston. What year is it?"

"2013, right?"

Julie and Dr. Wakefield shared a look, which she didn't like. She wanted Jake. She wanted out of this hospital. She wanted him right now.

"When is Jake going to get here?" she asked. Because she'd been awake for almost two weeks and he hadn't shown up yet. She didn't understand why, but she was sure that if Jake wasn't here, there had to be a good reason.

"Skye," Julie said, "can you remember where Jake is?"

"He was…" He'd been somewhere. Somewhere else. But why? Something pulled at her memory, but it wasn't even a slippery noodle she couldn't keep a grip on. It was more like a thin line of smoke that vanished as soon as she tried to touch it. "I don't know." She hated this feeling, of not knowing what was going on. "His company is just starting to take off. Maybe he got that job in New York? But I thought he'd be back by now…"

"That's all right," Dr. Wakefield said in a comforting tone. "Do you remember Grace?"

Skye frowned. They were *always* asking her about Grace. Did she remember Grace? No. Did she remember everyone—the doctors, her sister—asking about Grace? Yes. "She's my daughter."

The words made her want to cry. Her baby—the baby she'd wanted for *so* long—and Skye had no recollection of her at all. She didn't know if her own child was chubby or had hair or looked like Jake or *anything* about her. Just that Grace was her daughter.

"Is the baby okay? Am I well enough to hold her now?"

Dr. Wakefield pressed along her head. There was one area along the side that was still tender. "We have a physical therapy protocol for patients in a coma to keep their muscles from atrophying, but you've lost a lot of strength. You should be able to hold Grace as long as you're sitting, with pillows to help bolster your arms." He gave her an apologetic smile. "It'll be some time before you can carry her. I'm sorry about that, Skye."

"That's all right," she said. "As long as I can

hold her." She couldn't help it—her eyes started to drift shut. "When can I go home?"

"Soon," Dr. Wakefield said. He sounded as if he meant it. "We'll start the process of releasing you to your next of kin."

"That's Jake," she said, yawning. "Can you call him for me? I want him."

"Of course," Julie said in a soothing voice. "I'm sure it won't be long—*oh*!"

At this, Skye's eyes opened and there he was. *Jake*.

He looked so, so good. But…there was something off about him, too. Somehow, he looked older than she remembered—more fine lines around his eyes, thinner in the face.

*"Skye?"* He stood there, his mouth open. If she didn't know any better, she'd say he was in shock. "Oh, my God—are you all right?"

"Jake!" she cried in pure joy. "Oh, thank heavens—I was beginning to think you'd forgotten about me. Where have you been? I've missed you so much." She held up her arms, which took some effort. But he was worth it. God, she was *so* glad to see him.

He turned to the doctor. "Is she all right? I don't want to hurt her."

Julie gave Jake a warm smile. "Go on, you won't hurt her. Just be gentle."

"All right." He walked to the side of the bed and sat in the chair, staring at her as if he'd never seen her before. He took one of her hands in his. "It's good to see you."

"We'll leave you two alone," the doctor said. *Dr. Wakefield*, she mentally corrected. So she wouldn't forget. "Mr. Holt, when you're finished visiting, my research assistant Julie here or one of the nurses can give you the list of things Skye will need to transition to a home environment. She'll be ready to be released in a day or two."

"Sure," Jake said. He didn't sound quite right. Why was he acting so...oh, what was the word? So—so aloof.

Then they were alone.

"I am glad to see you," he told her, rubbing his thumb over his knuckles.

"I'm glad to see *you*. I dreamed of you all the time."

"That's...good." He swallowed nervously as he

stared at where their hands were joined. "What, exactly, did you dream?"

"It—well—I don't know if I have the words. I lose words sometimes. Like *aloof*." His eyebrows jumped up as he looked at her quizzically. "Just as an example," she added, feeling silly. Jake wasn't necessarily being aloof. She was pretty sure this was the first time she'd seen him, after all.

Then she realized what the problem was. "I must look awful," she said with a grimace. "If I'd known you were going to get here today, I'd have done...something." Point of fact, she couldn't actually remember the last time she'd showered and there was a section of her hair that had been shaved off.

"No, no—you look fine," Jake said. He gave her an off-kilter smile. "Feels like it's been a long time."

"I'm sorry," she said as she held out her other hand to him and, after what felt like two beats too many, he took it in his. "I've been asleep for so long..."

"Don't be sorry. It was an accident," he said firmly. "The important thing now is that you're awake. How are you? Is there anything I can do for you?"

"I haven't seen Grace. Is she okay?"

"Yes," Jake said. "You'll get to see her soon. But tell me more about how you are. What did you dream?"

"Really, just a bunch of images, you know? Things we did." She grinned at him. "Where we did them."

"Oh." His cheeks shot a deep red. "Those were good things. And good places."

She leaned toward him. He did look different from how she'd seen him in her dreams. Had he always been this thin? She couldn't be sure.

Well, that didn't matter. She was awake and he was here. Soon, they'd get Grace. That was all that counted right now. It wasn't that she wanted to spend more time in bed—there'd been enough of that—but if she remembered right, they could do just fine without a bed. "When you talk to the doctor, ask how long before I can do certain *things*, okay?" She waggled her eyebrows at him.

"Sure." He squeezed her hands and gave her another tight smile. Then, finally, he leaned over and did what she'd been waiting for—he kissed her.

Except it was a small kiss, a mere brushing of his lips against hers. Not a passionate, soul-consuming kiss. Not the kiss she'd dreamed about.

Why not?

"I'm going to go check on Grace," Jake said when the too-short kiss was over. "Your sister has her."

"Yes, Lark. Because you weren't here?" She shook her head, which was not the best idea she'd ever had. Her head began to hurt. "I missed something, didn't I? You had a job in New York, right?"

"New York?" He looked at her as if she'd sprouted a second head. Or maybe a third one. Oh, what she wouldn't give for a haircut—a good one—right about now. She wanted him to look at her with the love he'd always had in his eyes. "I did have a job there."

Oh, good—she'd gotten that part right. Suddenly, she was tired—the excitement of Jake's arrival had worn off, apparently. She yawned and tried to hide it behind her hand, but she didn't do a very good job. "Sorry," she mumbled. "I'm just so tired of being asleep."

Finally, Jake looked at her with the tenderness she recognized. "Well, I'm here now. I'll talk to the doctor and do what I need to in order to get you set up." He leaned over and kissed her on the forehead. "You rest up. Grace needs you to get better."

"Okay," she agreed, having trouble keeping her eyes open. "But you'll come back for me, right?"

There was another one of those long pauses as he stared at her. "I will *always* come back for you, Skye." He squeezed her hand. "Now get some rest. I'll see you soon. I promise."

"Good," she told him as she squeezed back. Then his warmth was away from her.

Jake was here, she thought as she drifted. He was going to get Grace. And he'd come back for her.

Everything was going to be perfect.

# Two

"What's wrong with her?"

Both the doctor and his research assistant looked at Jake with raised eyebrows. Okay, maybe that had been a little gruff—but seriously?

She was different. Or rather, she was the same as she'd once been—but not the same woman she'd been the last time he'd seen her. Skye hadn't looked at him with that kind of adoration in a long time. And when was the last time she'd wanted sex? When was the last time she'd *wanted* him?

Jake had only taken one job in New York. And that had been two years ago. It'd been a small job, but it'd led to bigger and better things.

Two years ago. That'd been the last time things

had been good between them. After Jake had started getting those bigger and better jobs, things had begun to fall apart.

"Skye had a traumatic brain injury," the doctor explained. "I'm her surgeon. Dr. Lucas Wakefield," he added, sticking out his hand.

Jake shook it. "But what does that mean?"

"It means that, as near as we can tell, Skye was driving into Royal when the tornado hit. We suspect her car was picked up and tossed around."

*"And?"* Jake demanded. Julie's eyebrows went up again, but Jake was past caring.

Skye had driven into a damn tornado. Why? That wasn't like her. She was more careful than that. She knew how Texas weather could be. She would have taken shelter or gotten off the road or something.

"Think of it as a concussion—only the most extreme kind. We kept her under for a few months to allow her brain to heal and it took her some time to wake up after we cut back on the drugs we were using to induce the coma. Her memory is…compromised."

"And what does *that* mean?" Jake demanded.

What was it going to take to get a straight answer out of the man?

"She's got what the layperson might call amnesia," Dr. Wakefield explained. "She doesn't seem to have the last two years, although her long-term memory is mostly intact. Anything that happened right before the accident is probably gone for good."

For the second time that day, Jake had to lean on something to keep his legs underneath him. "Will she—will she get those two years back?" Would she remember how things had broken between them? Would she remember the fight? The divorce papers?

When he'd seen her just now, she hadn't had her ring on. She hadn't had her earrings in, either—the big diamond studs he'd bought her just as things had started to go south on them. He wondered where they were—lost in the storm or left behind on purpose?

"Hard to say. The brain is an amazing organ. For now, we recommend keeping any shocks to the system to a bare minimum. Obviously, she knows about your daughter."

Grace. *His* daughter, Grace.

"But," Dr. Wakefield went on as if Jake weren't on the verge of collapse, "if there were…other surprises, I'd keep those close to the vest."

"You want me to, what—lie to her?"

Julie said, "Not lie, no. Think of it as glossing over. She's going to be confused for some time. Too much too soon would be a severe shock to her system. We don't want her to have a setback."

Jake shook his head, hoping to get the world to stop spinning. None of this was right. None of it.

Skye didn't remember how they'd broken up. Why they'd broken up.

And he couldn't tell her.

God, what a mess.

Julie handed him a packet. "She'll have to do physical therapy to regain her muscle strength. This is a preliminary list of stretches and exercises you'll need to help her with at home during her recovery to rebuild her strength to a point where PT will be helpful to her. In a week or two, you'll need to bring her into the office so she can work with a therapist."

He stared at the sheet. The top one had a photo of a woman in a spandex unitard laying on the floor and another woman in hospital scrubs stretching her leg so that it pointed straight up. "Me?"

"Are you two married?" Julie eyed him. Closely. "If so, you're her next of kin. We had planned to release her to Lark Taylor, but if you're here, you'll be the one in charge of her care."

"We are married," he said, feeling the full impact of those words. He'd sworn vows to her, vows to be there for her in sickness and in health, until death parted them. She'd wanted to break those vows, but because she'd been in a coma and he'd been in a different hemisphere, they hadn't managed to do that just yet.

Then something else dawned on him. "I suppose you're going to tell me that I can't take her back to Houston?"

"That wouldn't be wise," Dr. Wakefield said, giving Jake a suspicious look. "I'd like to continue to monitor her recovery. I have colleagues in Houston that I could refer you to, but I'd prefer to remain her primary. Consistency of care can't be overestimated at this point."

He was going to have to take care of her. He was going to have to look at her and know he'd lost her and not tell her that. He couldn't tell her about the slow way the spark had died or how she'd had him served with papers.

Instead, he was going to have to take care of a woman who thought she still loved him because she couldn't remember how she'd stopped loving him.

And to do that, he was going to have to stay in the pit that was Royal, Texas.

How could this get any worse?

Jake had broken the cardinal rule. No matter how bad things were, never, *ever* ask how they could possibly be worse.

Because a man never knew when a dog was going to try and break through the door to get to him.

Jake stood on the front porch of a nondescript house in a nice part of town. He was pretty sure this was the address Keaton had given him. On the other side of the door, the dog was howling and scratching like a crazed beast. Jake debated getting back in the car. If the dog got out, Jake would prefer to have a layer of metal between the two of them.

Seconds ticked by more slowly than molasses

in January. His fingers started twitching toward the doorbell to ring it again. They knew he was coming, right?

The dog still going nuts, Jake was just about to start pounding on the door when he heard the lock being turned. "Nicki!" Keaton shouted. "Knock it off! Back up!"

The barking ceased almost immediately, then the door cracked open and the first thing Jake heard was the wailing of a baby. An unhappy baby.

"About time," Keaton grumbled, opening the door and standing aside. "You woke her up. Next time, just knock. That doesn't seem to set Nicki off nearly as badly as the doorbell does."

"Sorry." And truthfully—with all that screaming? Jake actually *was* sorry.

Keaton got the door closed behind him. Jake's eyes took a moment to adjust to the dim lighting. The blinds were down and in addition to the screaming he heard the sounds of...classical music?

"This way," Keaton said, stepping around Jake. "Watch out for Nicki."

Jake eyed the dog that was now sitting next to

the door. The dog's hackles were up and it was growling, but at least it hadn't attacked. "Nice doggie," Jake said as he stepped around the animal. Man, he hoped that thing was well trained. "Good girl."

"Yeah, we just got her a few weeks ago. Australian shepherd. Nicki goes with me out to the ranch—I'm training her to keep tabs on the cattle. She's really good at it." As Keaton spoke, he walked confidently though the house. He led Jake—and Nicki—past large framed landscapes of Texas in all the seasons—bluebells in one, the bright summer sky in another. They walked past shelves that seemed to overflow with books, all of which looked uniformly well-read. This was not the pristine, almost sterile kind of house that Skye had grown up in. This was a home that seemed lived in. But it didn't seem particularly feminine.

"This your place?" he asked, trying to keep his tone casual.

"It's Lark's. We're building a place of our own." Keaton didn't offer any more details.

Jake had a lot of questions from that one statement, but before he could figure out how to ask them, they entered a room that had probably once been a tidy great room. Except now there were baby blankets draped everywhere, mats with mirrored things attached spread over the floor and more stuffed animals than Jake could count. There were bookshelves in here, too, but the books had been cleared off the lower ones and bins full of toys and things that Jake didn't recognize now filled the space. Plus, there was an absolutely huge television along one wall that seemed out of place in the worst sort of way.

In the middle of it all, on a couch that was piled high with cloths and diapers, sat Skye's sister, Lark, with a small, squalling baby in her arms. Lark was wearing medical scrubs. Maybe she was a nurse?

At the sight of them, Lark got a mean look about her—a look Jake recognized from days long gone. It was a look he'd seen more often on Vera Taylor's face than on Skye's, but the hatred was unmistakable.

"Babe," Keaton said, crouching down in front of her. He rubbed his hands over her thighs. "You remember Jake, my—my brother?"

"No," Lark said. But it didn't sound as if she was answering Keaton's question.

"Lark," Jake said, trying to be polite about it.

The baby cried even more. Jake wouldn't have thought that was possible, but it was. This morning, he hadn't been a father. Now he was faced with a wailing infant.

Skye wasn't supposed to have any shocks to her system. He wished someone had given the same orders for him because he wasn't sure how much more he could take.

"Where have you *been*?" Lark snapped. Her eyes filled with tears, and Jake noticed the dark circles underneath.

"Babe…" Keaton said, touching her face. It was a tender gesture.

Jake wasn't sure what part of this scene made the least amount of sense. Keaton had always said Lark Taylor was a stuck-up bookworm who thought she was better than everyone else—and Jake had never argued that point much. Lark hadn't liked Jake. The feeling had been mutual.

"I was in Bahrain. I came back for Skye and for our daughter." The words were coming easier now. But he stared at the little baby still crying in Lark's arms and the room began to feel smaller.

"Oh," Lark said. "So glad to see that you've decided to acknowledge her. Where have you been since she was born? Do you even know how old she is? Do you know *anything* about her?"

Before Jake could reply, Keaton spoke. "Lark," he said in a soft voice, trying to draw her attention back to him. "We talked about this."

"But you know him, Keaton. You *know* he's going to take Grace and disappear. Just like he always does."

Yeah, that stung. "I promise, I'm not going to walk off with that baby."

"Because you keep your promises, right?" Lark shot back at him. The baby was really letting loose now. "I wouldn't trust you farther than I can throw you."

Okay, that stung more. Jake nervously eyed the baby—his daughter—and fought the urge to cover his ears. Unfamiliar panic began to build in his chest. "I don't know where you think I'm going to go with an infant, not when Skye's doctor insists she needs to stay local. Despite what you assume about me and Skye, I do *not* disappear. I had a job in Bahrain, but it's over now. I'm *going* to take care of my family."

Keaton and Lark exchanged a look. Jake couldn't

take his eyes off the baby. She was small and bald and an interesting shade of red—although he hoped that was from all the screaming and not her natural color. "How old is she?"

"Three months." Lark began rocking and patting the baby on the back. She wasn't looking at Jake, but that was okay. At least she was telling him what he needed to know. "She was eleven weeks premature—that's their best guess. She was in the NICU for two months. And since Skye was still under when Grace was ready to leave the hospital, she was turned over to her next of kin." She looked at Keaton. The anger she'd directed at Jake was gone from her eyes; now he saw something else there. "That's us."

Jake recognized the emotion. Lark looked at Keaton the way Skye used to look at him. It'd been a while, though.

He sat in a nearby recliner and dropped his head into his hands, trying to keep his emotions in check. When had Skye stopped looking at him like that? And why hadn't he noticed when she did?

"Since she was so early," Lark went on, "she's got a bunch of health risks that full-term babies don't have to worry about. She shouldn't be out-side in this weather and she shouldn't be around strangers. If she got sick, she could wind up back in the hospital. Or worse. She's a full-time job right now."

Jake knew that shaking his head wasn't going to help a damn thing but he did it anyway. He had jobs waiting now—Bahrain had been very good for him. He couldn't take an infant with health risks out of the country. Hell, he couldn't even take Skye to Houston.

Trapped. He was trapped in this town.

"Keaton said he told you about the blood tests," Lark said into the silence.

"He did."

"He said you didn't know about Grace."

"I thought…" He didn't know what to do. His entire world—everything he *thought* he knew—had been turned inside out in the space of about four hours.

He didn't trust his brother and he didn't trust the Taylors—with the exception of Skye.

He thought that his brother would never trust a Taylor either. Yet here Jake sat, in Lark Taylor's house, watching her and Keaton cuddle and soothe a fussy baby. Together.

"What did you think?" For the first time since Jake had walked into this house, he heard the attitude in Keaton's voice.

He didn't want to tell them this. But his back was against a wall—a wall covered in four-inch spikes. As much as he hated it, he needed both Lark and Keaton right now. He had a bunch of questions and they had the closest thing to answers.

"Skye and I…" He absolutely could *not* tell them about the divorce papers. "I had that big job in Bahrain coming up. It was a yearlong contract and she decided she didn't want to spend that much time in a foreign country. Bahrain may be richer than sin, but it's not exactly a progressive state."

All of that was true enough. She hadn't wanted to go to Bahrain and she hadn't wanted to stay home alone. She'd wanted him to stay with her. And he'd picked the job over her. That had been the proverbial straw that had broken the camel's back.

"Is that it?" Keaton said with a snort.

"Yes." And since Skye might never remember the fight, there was no one to contradict Jake's lie.

Lark looked victorious, but strangely, it didn't make her seem any happier. "Were you married? Skye said you were but she didn't have her ring on and who knows, with that memory of hers." She looked at Jake's hand.

Jake spun the plain gold band around his finger. It'd been the only ring they'd been able to afford when they slipped off into the night together four years ago.

"Yes. We got married three days after we left."

Silence followed this statement. He and Skye had driven to Houston and found a preacher who would marry them. He'd been wearing his old boots and a pair of jeans, but Skye had been in a simple white skirt and a bright blue top. She'd been so beautiful that day...

"So what are you going to do now?" Keaton finally asked. "Because Lark is right. We're not going to stand aside and let you disappear off into the night with this baby. We're not going to let you do anything that would put her at risk."

Jake gritted his teeth. He had no choice but to stay here. He looked at the baby girl. She was still crying—but at least now the decibel level wouldn't shatter glass. Jake tried to smile at the baby, but the terror the tiny baby—his *daughter*, for crying out loud!—was sparking in his chest was making breathing difficult.

He'd never held a baby before. He didn't have the first idea how to do any of the basics—bottles and diapers and everything else. He and Skye had wanted to wait.

That wasn't true. Skye had wanted a baby from the very beginning. But Jake had looked at the reality of being a young couple barely scraping by and he'd convinced her that they needed to wait until their financial situation was more secure.

That was another thing she'd thrown back in his face during the fight, another ultimatum she'd issued. Have a baby or it's over.

He'd said after the Bahrain job. He was going to make a fortune in Bahrain. Another year, and they'd be set.

"Skye is going to be released to my care, maybe tomorrow."

"Are you going to be able to take care of her?"

Jake would have normally taken umbrage at his

brother's attitude, but right now? Yeah, it was a danged good question.

"I don't know."

Near silence descended upon the room. "We could keep her," Lark finally said, looking at the baby.

"What?"

"We could keep Grace—just until Skye gets settled. Keaton and I know her schedule. We know how to take care of her. She shouldn't be out in this weather, anyway, not until she's stronger. That way, you can focus on getting Skye back into shape. You can bring Skye over here to visit the baby, but she won't have to get up in the middle of the night."

Could he do that? This was his daughter. A daughter he'd only known about for…five hours, but still—his flesh and blood.

He didn't want to be a monster about this. This wasn't him abandoning the baby. This was him getting Skye to the point where she could take over, right?

Plus, if he left Grace here, that would prove that he wasn't going to skip town again. "Would that be okay? I don't want to impose, but the sooner we can get Skye back to full strength, the better."

Lark sighed as she looked at Grace. "Keaton and I already have it all worked out and, really, she's an angel."

"I'll need to get a house of my own. The whole point of you keeping the baby here is to give Skye room to recover at her own pace." To put it less tactfully, he didn't want to sleep under the same roof as Keaton and Lark—even if they were being really good to Grace.

"You're actually going to stay?" Keaton sounded doubtful.

Jake let the comment slide. "Skye's doctors are here and I'm not going to do a damn thing that might set her back. I know you don't believe this, but I didn't know about the tornado until this morning. Hell, I don't even know if Mom and Dad came through all right." If he'd known...

"Mom and Dad are okay," Keaton said in a quiet voice. "Some property damage. The ranch house is being rebuilt, but they were in Florida and Alabama, checking out some retirement properties, so they weren't in the line of the storm. We've had them over a few times."

"Good. I'm glad." Strangely, he was. He'd spent the last four years pointedly not caring about what his family was doing. They'd wanted him to put the family above Skye. Nothing was more important to him than Skye.

"They adore Grace," Lark said in a way that made it pretty clear that this absolved most of their sins in her eyes.

"And they've come to see that Lark is nothing like her parents," Keaton went on. "I think they're realizing that not all Taylors are lying, cheating dogs."

Bitterness rose up in the back of Jake's throat. Oh, sure—now his parents were going to open their arms and welcome a Taylor into the family. But not for Jake and Skye when he had needed them to.

"What about your parents?" he asked Lark.

She dropped her eyes. "They're…okay. Fine."

"Whit Daltry's got some houses for rent in Pine Valley," Keaton said, changing the subject. "I think a couple of them are furnished—not too far from here. I'll call him."

"Thanks. That'd be great." He was not buying a house. He was not staying in Royal long. Just long enough to get Skye back on her feet and figure out where they stood.

Just then, the baby made a little hiccup-sigh noise that pulled at his heartstrings.

Lark shifted Grace off of her shoulder. Keaton picked the baby up so smoothly that Jake was jealous. "Grace, honey—this is your daddy," Keaton said as he rubbed her on her back. Then, to Jake, he added, "You ready?"

Not really—but Jake wasn't going to admit that to Keaton. He tried to cradle his arms in the right way. Then Keaton laid the baby out in them.

The world seemed to tilt off its axis as Jake looked down into his daughter's eyes. They were a pale blue—just like her mother's. Up close now, he could see that Grace had wispy hairs on her head that were so white and fine they were almost see-through.

She didn't start bawling, which he took as a good sign. Instead, she waved her tiny hands around, so of course he had to offer her one of his fingers. When she latched on to it, he felt lost and yet *not* lost at the same time.

He was responsible for this little girl from this moment until the day he drew his last breath. The weight of it hit him so hard that, if he hadn't already been sitting, his knees would have buckled.

This was his daughter. He and Skye had created this little person.

God, he wished she were here with him. That they could have done this together. That things between them had been different. That he'd been different.

But he couldn't change the past, not when his present—and his future—was gripping his little finger with surprising strength.

"Hi, Grace," he whispered. He shook his hand a little, raising her fist with his pinkie finger. "It's so good to meet you."

The baby smiled, which made Jake feel ten feet tall. "Hey, she's smiling at—"

Then a horrible noise—and an even more horrible smell—cut him off.

Keaton began to laugh. The dog whined and put its paws over its nose.

"Sorry," Lark said, rising quickly. "She's about due for another bottle, too."

"Time for your first lesson—diapers," Keaton said as he clapped Jake on the back. "Welcome to fatherhood."

# Three

"Grace is with Lark, right?" Skye asked. She knew Jake had answered that question at least three times already, but she wanted to see her daughter.

"Are you asking because you don't remember the answer or because you don't trust me?" Jake grinned at her from the driver's seat. It was an easy grin that warmed her from the inside out—but there was something underneath it that had an edge.

She was going home. With Jake. The past few days had been the longest of her waking life. Skye had been ready and willing to leave that hospital far behind and get back to making new memories with Jake.

"I just…I just want to see her again. I remember you already said yes," she hurried to add. "I feel like I've missed so much." She laughed. "Probably because I have."

The process of being released from the hospital had taken most of the day. Late winter twilight settled over the landscape as Jake drove toward their new home. "And…we're not going back to our apartment, right?"

"That's right," he said gently. "The doctor wants you to stay close to the hospital. I rented a house. It's close to Lark and the baby and not too far from the hospital."

"I wish I remembered Grace," she said, an impotent frustration bubbling up. "Why is Lark keeping her?"

"Because Lark is a nurse and you need to recover," he answered smoothly. "We'll go over and visit, I promise. And I always keep my promises, don't I?"

"Yes…" She tried to make sense of that hidden edge to his words It was almost as if he was mad at her. But did that make any sense?

No, it didn't. He was probably just upset that she'd been hurt so badly. Jake had never been the best at expressing his feelings. She knew there were holes in her memory and she didn't know if those holes would ever get filled.

But she was still here and she was getting better. She'd just have to make some new memories with Jake. And with Grace.

She looked around and was surprised to see that she recognized the road they were on. "Stop!" she cried, feeling hopeful. Now was as good a time as any to start making some of those new memories.

"What?" Jake asked in alarm as he slammed on the brakes. His right arm flew across her chest to keep her from lurching forward.

"We used to park here, remember?" She undid her seat belt and slid over to him. "We used to stop here on the way home."

She grinned nervously at him. Yes, she wanted to get home, but she'd been in a bed—by herself—for the last four months. Four months without Jake. It was time to fix that starting right *now*.

Jake did not bend much in her arms. She ran her fingers through his hair and pulled him down to her. "We did stop here, didn't we? I didn't get that wrong, did I?"

"We did," he said through gritted teeth.

"Are you going to kiss me, Jake Holt?" she whispered against his lips.

He turned his head. "The doctor said—he said we shouldn't stress you out too much. Physically."

Skye sighed in disappointment. "Not even if I want to be stressed? Just a little? Not even a kiss?"

Jake didn't reply for a moment. Then he sort of chuckled and said, "When we used to stop here, I don't remember it ever being *just* a kiss."

Skye leaned into him, feeling his warmth. The hospital had been cold. But Jake had always run hot. She'd loved curling up against him in the middle of winter, letting his body warm hers until things started to get downright steamy.

"I've missed you so much," she told him. It felt like an important thing to say. She was pretty sure she'd said it before, but she wanted to say it again.

He didn't respond. Not the way she'd hoped. Instead, he said, "Sorry, traffic. Can you buckle up? I don't want another car accident. I just got you out of that hospital." He said it in a jokey kind of way, as if she was supposed to laugh along with him. But she didn't.

"All right. But later I'm going to kiss you. I don't care what the doctors said."

"Later," he agreed. He waited until she was buckled up and then he drove on.

"How long will we be in Royal?" she asked. "I know how much you hate it here. I wish you didn't have to stay just because of me."

He tensed. "Aren't you glad to be back home?"

"I guess…" He shot her a worried look. "What?"

"I thought you'd be glad to be here, that's all. You'd talked about coming home—remember?"

"Oh, I know. I wish our families would see the light of day and put the feud to rest." She sighed. She was missing something again. It was as if there were a fog over her mind that was so thick that it hid things from her. But when she tried to grab it or push it aside, it slipped through her fingers. It was both there and *not* there. Just like her memory, apparently. "But I'd rather be with you than deal with my parents. Have you seen them? I don't think I have. I've seen Lark. And I want to say that… Didn't Lark come in and talk to me? While I was sick? She's with Keaton now, right?"

"Yeah, that's right." He gave her a tight smile.

"Good. I'm glad. I knew the Taylors and the Holts could get along if they just…just…oh, shoot. I lost another word."

"It's okay," Jake said quickly. "I understand what you mean. Hey—here we are."

Jake turned past a big sign that announced they were in Pine Valley. They drove past spacious homes set far back from the road.

"Is this where we're going to stay? This is nice," Skye said, glancing out the window.

"I wanted to get the best for you," he told her. "This is a furnished house, but if there's something you want from the apartment back in Houston…" His voice trailed off. "Or I can buy you new things, too. Money is no object."

"Since when?" she demanded. "I mean, we were just getting comfortable. I don't think we should drain the bank accounts dry."

"Oh. Um, well—hmm. The last job," he said, stumbling over the words. "I, uh, I did a great job and I got a huge bonus."

"You did? Oh, Jake—that's wonderful!" But then confusion set in again. "Is that why you weren't with me? In the accident? Because of the job?"

"Yeah. This is it." He pulled into a long drive. "This house has a small gym in it. That's why I picked it. That way you can use a couple of machines to help you regain your strength."

"Oh, good thinking." Because the one thing she did not have right now was a lot of strength. She hated feeling weak, but she wouldn't be that way for long.

Jake parked and Skye undid her belt again. She got the door open as he went around the front of the car, but when she slid out of the seat, her legs almost didn't hold. "Whoa," she gasped, clinging to the door for support. She'd gotten out of the bed on her own, but the rest of the trip had been in a wheelchair. She hadn't realized how weak she actually was.

"Easy, now," Jake said. "I've got you."

The next thing she knew, he swept Skye up into his strong arms as if she weighed nothing at all.

She giggled as he carried her up the steps to the front door. "It's like we're married," she said, resting her head against his shoulder.

"Yeah," he said. He sounded unconvincing. "Just like that. I carried you over the threshold of that hotel the night we got married, didn't I?"

"Mmm." Without loosening her grip, she twirled one finger through the short hairs on the back of his neck. "That was a good night, wasn't it? You were so handsome."

Jake set her down long enough to get the door open. Then, after the barest moment of hesitation, he picked her up again. "And you were beautiful," he said, sounding very serious about it. "You still are."

She laughed again. God, she'd missed this man. "I really need a shower before I'm going to start buying that line from you." Which was not a half-bad idea. "Or a bath? What does this place have? I think I'd need a bench in a shower."

"Your choice. There's a whirlpool tub that'll be good for soaking and a separate shower. I think it has a bench in it." He carried her over the threshold. "Welcome home, Skye."

"Oh, wow." Dusky light streamed in from floor-to-ceiling windows, illuminating a massive, well-appointed great room with leather furnishings and a comfortable-looking couch. Along one wall was a stone hearth. Skye craned her neck and saw that the great room opened onto a kitchen. She couldn't see much of it, but she caught glimpses of gleaming stainless steel and granite counter-tops. "Jake, this place is gorgeous! Are you sure we can afford it?"

"It was a big bonus," he told her. He carried her over to the comfortable couch and gently set her down. He tried to stand, but she wasn't going to let him go.

She held tight and pulled him down. He didn't fall into her the way he normally did, but he didn't pull away. "I missed you. This," she told him as she brushed her lips against his. "Feels like it's been forever."

"Yeah," he agreed. He pressed his lips to hers and sighed. Skye knew that noise. He always did that when he was ready and willing to take things to the next level. The first time he'd sighed against her mouth like that, she'd pulled away and demanded to know what was wrong, what she'd messed up. And instead of telling her she wasn't a good kisser, he'd only pulled her in closer and kissed her hard.

So she opened her mouth and traced her tongue over his lips and waited for him to take the next step.

He didn't.

He stood up and damn it all, she wasn't strong enough to hold on to him. "Um, yeah. Don't want to overdo it on your first night home."

She frowned at him. "You won't break me, you know."

"I know, I know. Hey, are you hungry? I could order some food. I drove past the Tower Pizza—it's still standing. I'll get you a green pepper and mushroom."

"Oh. Okay." Something still felt...off. She groped around in her mind, trying to get the fog that had covered everything to shift or just go the heck away, but it didn't. "But you don't like mushrooms. You don't have to eat them just for my sake."

He paused halfway to the kitchen. "I'll get two pizzas. I know you don't like pepperoni. Then we can have some for lunch tomorrow. Sound good?"

She snickered at him. "Two pizzas? That must have been some bonus."

A shadow crossed over his face. But he said, "It was. I'll be right back. Then we'll see about getting you into the shower."

Skye liked the sound of that. She looked down at her loose-fitting yoga pants and unisex T-shirt emblazoned with the hospital's logo on it. This was not a good look—in fact, she probably resembled an escaped mental patient more than anything else.

She just wanted to put this whole brain-injury thing behind them and get back to their lives. And Grace—she needed to get Grace, although the concept of a small human that was her daughter wasn't something she had a firm grasp on just yet. Grace Holt was still…an abstract idea.

They'd get to Grace. Lark had the baby so Skye felt okay just focusing on Jake right now.

It really did feel like longer than a few months since she'd been with him. But her dreams had been wild and varied and had always had a glimmer of something that might have been a memory at the core of them—like parking at that spot and making out.

That settled it. Shower first, real clothing second, seducing Jake third.

She was going to remember this.

Jake stood in the kitchen, forcing himself to breathe evenly.

Jesus, she was going to kill him. He was halfway amazed he wasn't already dead yet.

What the hell was going on? That doctor hadn't been lying when he'd said that Skye had lost the past two years. It was as if the whole seven hundred and thirty days hadn't happened. The Skye that was sitting out there on that couch was the Skye he'd run away with—bold and forward and unable to keep her hands off of him. She was the Skye he'd been unable to stay away from, come hell or high water.

Gone was the quiet, distant woman who didn't care how much he hated this town, didn't want to share a pizza with him—didn't want *him*. The Skye on the couch had no clue that other Skye had taken over the past two years of her life.

She didn't remember falling out of love with him.

She still thought she loved him.

And she seemed hell-bound to prove it.

What was he supposed to do here? The jerk move would be to just start sleeping with her. But the doctor seemed to think she'd start to recover some of her memories and once she did—once she remembered the divorce papers he'd shoved into his glove box—she'd accuse him of taking advantage of her while she was confused.

But she was throwing herself at him and damn it, his stupid body had apparently decided that, yeah, maybe they could *all* forget about the past two years and go back to how it'd been. Jake had fought himself to keep from kissing her back in the car.

And that kiss on the couch? God, she'd been warm and soft and inviting. He wanted to keep going, to remember those good times—like their wedding night—with her.

He was stuck between a rock and a very hard place.

Finally, he managed to will his body to stand down. He dialed Tower and ordered the pizzas, but they'd be almost forty-five minutes.

*Fine.* He could get Skye into the bathroom and close the door and...go run on the treadmill that was supposedly in the basement of this house to cool down.

He could not sleep with her. He *would* not, even though they were still technically married. Because it was just that—a technicality. The divorce papers that had been waiting for him had made her position on the matter of their marriage plenty clear. She might not love him like she once had, but he couldn't use her—even if she wanted to be used. When she remembered, she'd wind up hating him. And since they had a daughter to consider, he didn't want that, either.

When he was sure he could keep himself under control, he went back into the great room. "The pizza will be here in about—" He checked his watch. He'd been standing in the kitchen for a while. "Forty minutes. Do you want to have a bath first?"

"That would be great," she agreed with a glint in her eyes. He didn't like that glint. It spelled only one thing—trouble.

"Let's try walking this time," he said. He was supposed to make sure she exercised, right? And that would probably take a lot of energy. If he could make sure she was tired out—as the doctor recommended—then maybe she would stop throwing herself at him.

She scowled at him, as if she'd been counting on him carrying her everywhere. Well, too bad. He didn't need to feel her weight in his arms, her body pressed against his. Nope. Didn't need it at all. Not even a little.

Yeah, right.

He took hold of her hands and got her up on her feet. "You go first," he told her. "I'll be right behind you."

More scowling. "Can't you put your arm around me?"

"No." When she glared, he added, "The doctor said you had to use your muscles."

The disgruntled look faded into something that was worry instead. "If I fall…"

"I'll catch you," he told her. And he meant it.

He put his hands on her shoulders and turned her toward the stairs. The bathroom in the master suite was where he was headed—but it was at the far end of the house. What normally would have been a thirty-second trip took close to three minutes. He kept his hand on her back the whole time, so she'd know he was right there.

"Down the hall," he told her. "Keep going."

"This place…is a lot…bigger than our apartment," she puffed.

"You're almost there, Skye. You can do it." He said it because it seemed like the thing to say to someone who was working really hard. He could see sweat bead up on the back of Skye's neck as she took slow steps, her hands brushing against the wall for added support.

"Are we…there yet?" she panted.

"Into the bedroom," he instructed, guiding her with his hand.

"Thought you'd…never ask. Oh! Pretty!"

The bedroom was done in royal blues and warm golds, giving the whole thing a celestial feeling. A king-size bed was tucked into a wide bay window. To the left, there was another fireplace with a flat-screen television mounted over the mantle. On the right was their destination—the bathroom.

Skye had almost come to a complete stop. "Bath or shower?"

"Bath," came the weak reply.

Jake had her sit on the toilet while he got the water going. He took some towels from under the sink and laid them where she could reach them. "Okay," he said as he checked to make sure that the shampoo and soap were within easy reach. "You bathe and I'll be back to check on you in— what's wrong?"

He asked because Skye had sighed heavily and her lip was quivering. He knew what that meant—she was trying not to cry. "I don't know if I can get in by myself," she said in a low whisper. "I'm sorry."

"Don't be, babe." Although he was pretty sorry, too. This was going to be torture, pure and simple. Because he saw immediately what he was going to have to do—strip those clothes off of her and get her into the tub.

And if she was hard to resist when she was dry and clothed, how was he going to keep his hands to himself when she was naked and wet?

He pulled the oversize T-shirt off of her and was nearly knocked off his feet. She wasn't wearing a bra. She'd never really needed one—so he shouldn't have been surprised. Still, to be suddenly confronted with her breasts was doing very little to help his resolve.

"I need you. To stand," he forced himself to say. "So I can get you out of those pants. And into the tub."

She looked up at him and managed a beautiful blush. But she held out her hands for him to pull her up. When he got her on her feet, she looped her arms around his neck and let him carry most of her weight.

"It'll…it'll get better, right?"

"Absolutely," he agreed, trying to figure out how to get the pants off without touching her bottom. "You're already so much better than you were yesterday. Think about how good you're going to feel tomorrow."

Finally, he gave up. The pants were loose, but not so loose that they'd just fall right off her hips. He had to skim his hands down over her skin. And down. And down.

He found himself eye to eye with the V where her legs met. There'd been a time—say, about two or three years ago—when he'd have taken every single advantage of this position and lavished attention on her body.

But he didn't now. He *couldn't*. He absolutely could not take advantage of a woman who wasn't entirely in her right mind. So he forced himself to stand.

She gave him a weak smile. "Takes you back, doesn't it?"

"It was a *great* honeymoon. Don't think we left the hotel room for three days," he told her as he half supported, half lifted her into the tub. "Easy," he cautioned as her foot slipped. "I've got you."

It'd been such a freeing thing—running away

from home, getting married and not caring a lick whether their parents approved or not. Jake had a new job and Skye had just graduated from college. They weren't little kids who were in "like" anymore. They'd become grown-ups who could do what they wanted, when they wanted. And what they'd wanted to do was each other.

So they had. For three straight days. That was their honeymoon.

It'd taken Jake eight months to pay off the cost of the hotel on their credit cards. And it'd been worth it.

Finally, Skye was settled into the tub. The water barely lapped over her nipples as she sank lower. "Mmm, this feels good," she murmured and that was enough to make breathing much more difficult for Jake.

He needed to get out of this bathroom and he needed to do it right now. But before he could say *I'll be back*, she asked, "Did you say this had jets?"

"Yeah." Which was fine. Figuring out the controls on the whirlpool was something to focus on besides her nude body. He got the jets going.

"Okay, I'll check on you in a few minutes to see if you need help getting out."

"But I…" He heard a small splash. "Jake, I'm tired. I don't think I can wash my hair."

God was punishing him. That had to be it. This was some sort of cosmic joke—divorce papers from the woman who suddenly loved him again.

He dropped his head. "Okay, but when the doorbell rings, it's the pizza and I'll have to go." Maybe he'd get lucky and the pizza would come much faster than advertised.

The tub had one of those fancy faucets that looked like an old-fashioned telephone, which was great and also really awful because he had no excuse not to help her. He could do this. He could take care of her while she was in the tub, and he wouldn't touch anything but her hair. He was a man of principle, damn it. He was not the horny teenager he'd once been. So what if he hadn't been with a woman since the last time with Skye? So what if that was ten months ago? He was master of his domain and his domain was currently closed for business.

So it was time to suck it up and keep his hands to himself. Or just confined to her hair. That was it. He wasn't even going to look at her breasts again. Nope.

He had to lean across the tub—and across her—to turn the tap back on. The water was still warm, but he let it run until it was the right temperature. Then—repeating *Not looking* to himself over and over—he moved the faucet over her head in slow, even strokes.

"Lean your head back," he told her and even he didn't miss how deep his voice had suddenly gotten. But he kept his eyes locked on her fine white hair.

It was nearly translucent when it was wet. He squeezed the shampoo into his hand and started on the side that hadn't been shaved. Slowly, he worked the shampoo into her hair.

The results were…not pretty. "Did you do this in the hospital?"

"I don't… No? I don't think so. Lark… Hmm. I think Lark did a dry shampoo? Is that a real thing?"

"Sure," he said. He rinsed her off. "I'm going to do that again, okay?"

"Okay, babe," she said. "It feels wonderful. Thank you so much."

She was leaning back, her eyes closed as he lathered and repeated a third time, just to be sure he didn't miss anything. Then he put in some conditioner. It helped to have a concrete task that required his attention. He absolutely did not want to hit the side where she'd cracked her head. The hospital had shaved the hair down, probably months ago. Right now, on one side she had the long, platinum white hair she'd worn since forever and on the other, a patch of hair that was only an inch and a half long. "This is a good look for you," he told her as he rinsed her again. "Almost punk. Very edgy."

"You like?" She sounded sleepy.

Good. Between the difficult trip up here and the warm, soothing bath, maybe she'd just crash out in bed and he could go sleep on the couch. He was not sleeping in the bed with her and that was final.

"It's different," he told her. "Okay, your hair is done. I'll just go wait for the pizza and…"

She opened her eyes and looked up at him and he knew he was so, *so* screwed. "But, babe…"

Maybe this was karma. He'd done something in a former life and now this life was balancing the scales or however that worked. He must have been a terrible person in that former life because this? This was going to drive him mad.

She hadn't had a real bath in months. She was tired and exhausted.

He had to wash her.

Deep breaths. Think of…oil drills. Computer interfaces. Cloud computing. Yes. Nothing sexy about that.

"Lean forward," he told her. She managed to pull herself up and hug her knees to her chest, resting her head so she could watch him.

"This isn't quite how the honeymoon went, is it?"

"Nope," he replied, all of his attention focused on the soap and the washcloth and…and the oppressive heat he'd lived through in Bahrain. Hot and dry and miserable. And he'd been alone. It'd been hell on earth.

His thoughts firmly centered on the furnace that was Bahrain, he began to wash her back.

Small circles. Back and forth. Getting months in a hospital off of her. Eyes only where they needed to be. Gently. Not too hard.

Other things were hard, though. To the point of pain.

He used the faucet to rinse off her back and shoulders. Then, because he didn't want to seem like a jerk, he said, "Need me to do your arms?"

She held one out and he repeated the process. *Eyes on the elbow,* he told himself as he worked on her body. He finished that arm, then did the other.

"Legs?"

Legs were harder. She leaned back and let her arms float in the water, which meant her breasts were right at the water line again. Plus, when she lifted one leg and set it on the side of the tub, it left him with a view he had trouble *not* admiring.

He resorted to mentally running through that old kid's song—*Hip bone connected to the thigh bone, thigh bone connected to the knee bone*—just because it gave his brain something to do.

Skye hummed. It was a sound of pleasure—relaxation and happiness and maybe a touch of eroticism as he massaged her skin. "God, I'm so glad you're here." She managed to wiggle her toes at him and damned if it didn't get his blood pumping fast.

*Okay*, he thought, adjusting his pants. *Faster*.

"Jake…" she said, soft and pretty.

The doorbell rang.

Thank God. "Pizza," he said. "I've got to pay the guy."

"I don't want to go back downstairs," she called out behind him. "It's too far away."

"I'll bring it up here. We'll watch TV and call it a date." The words were out before he realized they were leaving his mouth.

What the hell? He was not going to pretend it was a date. They didn't date, not anymore. They were in the process of splitting up and calling it a day. Hell, he shouldn't even be looking at her naked anymore, much less touching her. She was vulnerable. Her memory was compromised. He could not let an injured woman make bedroom eyes at him and he especially could not let the bedroom-eyes thing work.

As he hurried down the long hall toward the steps, he made a deal with himself. If she remembered the way things had fallen apart—and still wanted to try again—well, he'd try again. They had a daughter, after all.

But she had to remember. And as the doctor

himself had ordered, she had to remember on her own.

Which meant he was acting as her caregiver here. Not a husband.

Although they were still married.

God, what a problem.

He paid for the pizzas and found a roll of paper towels in the kitchen. Fine. Perfect. Their first year married, when he'd been building his business from scratch and Skye had been taking whatever graphic design job she could get, this actually had been their idea of a hot date. A rented DVD—a cheap one—and a pizza. It hadn't mattered that it was a cheap date. All that had mattered back then was that they were together.

As he headed back upstairs, he hoped like hell she was out of the tub and wearing…something. He didn't know what. Even those clothes she'd come home in would be better than nude. He was going to be strong, he really was. But he'd appreciate it if he didn't have to have his resolve tested on a second-by-second basis.

He hurried back to the bedroom and was crushed to see that the bed did not contain a fully clothed, dry Skye. "Skye?"

"I need help, please," she called out from the bathroom. "I'm…I'm afraid I'll slip and hit my head."

Dammit. He set the pizzas down on top of a dresser that was at the foot of the bed and, girding his loins as much as humanly possible, went back into the bathroom.

She was still naked.

Of course she was.

# Four

Jake stood in the doorway, staring down at her.

Skye shivered. The water was cooling off, but she was pretty sure that wasn't the reason why she was trembling.

No, it was the way he looked at her—with such *desperate* hunger that shivers raced over her body.

She just needed to hold him, to feel close to him again. She'd been alone in a bed for months. *Months.* She needed his warmth. She needed him.

She saw him swallow. "Let's get you out of there," he finally said.

She held out her hands and he pulled her to her feet. Water sluiced down her body, heightening her awareness. After the bathing massage he'd given her, every square inch of her skin felt alive and awake. It was a wonderful feeling, to know she was still alive.

"One foot at a time," he calmly instructed her as he took hold of her arms. "Easy does it."

She got out of the tub and stood still as he wrapped a big, fluffy towel around her. Then, he looked around and found a bathrobe hanging on the back of the door. "We'll use this. I'll try and get some clothes for you tomorrow. I can have someone go to the apartment and get your things, too." He sort of smiled at her. "I think this is the first time I've ever dressed you. Feels weird."

She laughed. "Definitely not normal," she agreed.

Once he had the robe belted around her waist— it was comically huge on her—he rubbed her hair dry. Well, really, half of her hair. He didn't get near the sore spot.

"Dinner is served," he said with a flourish when he was done.

Skye walked—slowly—out of the bathroom. She felt a million times better—clean and shiny and new.

"Here we go," Jake said, helping her sit on the

bed. He got the pizza, set the boxes in front of her and then sat on the other side.

Once they both had a slice, he asked, "Do you want to watch something?" He pointed to the big TV on the wall behind him.

"No, let's talk. I missed so much. How was the job?"

He looked down. "The job. It was good. A little more complicated than I anticipated, though."

"Is that why you got such a nice bonus?" Because this was a very nice house. Huge, yes—but that tub had been divine and the bedroom was gorgeous. They were certainly more comfortable than they'd been when they'd first gotten married. This place would have been out of their reach.

"Yeah," he said, studying his pizza. "Is yours good?"

"The best," she said, taking another bite. It wasn't glamorous or all that seductive but the pizza was quite possibly the best thing she'd ever eaten. "So, what's the plan?"

"The plan?"

"I mean, we're here, Lark has Grace. I wish she could be here with us, but I know it's not fair to ask you to take care of both of us."

"Um…yeah. The plan. Well, I'm still hammering out the details. Whit Daltry—he's the man I rented this house from—said we could go month-to-month. Your doctors want you to stay local, and I imagine that Grace's do, too. It might be a little while before I can get you back into the apartment."

Something about his answer wasn't right. But, try as she might, she couldn't identify what, exactly, was wrong about it. She didn't have much of an appetite left. "I guess I'm not used to real food," she told him, feeling sheepish and not knowing why. She'd only managed one piece, but he'd eaten almost half of his pizza.

"That's fine. I'll run it down to the fridge." He closed the box lids. "Let me get you tucked in. Tomorrow, we have to do some exercises and you're going to need your rest tonight." He cleared his throat. "I'll, uh, I'll sleep on the couch."

She stared at him. That definitely wasn't right. "What?"

"That way I won't bother you with my tossing and turning," he explained, as if this were a good enough reason for him to *not* sleep in the same bed with her. "And I have to do some work. I don't want to wake you up when I come in later."

"You're going to *work*? But I'm home now. I thought…"

"Skye," he said in a serious voice. "The doctor wants you to rest up. We'll have your exercises tomorrow, but otherwise you shouldn't be over-exerting yourself. You need to rest."

"But I'm tired of resting," she snapped. "I'm tired of being in bed alone. I'm here and you're here. I want *you*." When he didn't say anything, she added, "Don't you want me, too?"

"Of course I do. You're all I've ever wanted," he said, but it wasn't a declaration of love. It wasn't even a declaration of desire. It sounded like…an argument. One he'd had before. Had they fought? "But I'm not going to risk endangering your health for a little lust."

His words cut into her and she wasn't sure why. Lust? What about love? "Can't I at least *hold* you? I've dreamed of sleeping in your arms, Jake. I'm so tired of being in a bed alone." For some reason, she was on the verge of crying. She started blinking. "Please don't leave me alone."

He was glaring at her, as if she were stabbing

him in the back instead of asking for her husband to join her in the bedroom. "Is that what you really want?"

"Yes," she said as she wiped at her eyes. "I just want you. We don't have to fool around. You're right. I want to get better, faster. I just don't want to be alone tonight."

He got off the bed and picked up the pizza boxes. "Fine. But I need to log on and check a few things. After that, I'll come to bed." Then he left the room.

It should have felt like a victory, but it didn't. Why didn't he want to be with her? Why was this a fight?

Why had he rebuffed her advances at every single turn?

She dropped her head into her hands, which was not a smart thing to do. Her sore spot throbbed and, darn it all, she *was* exhausted.

Maybe Jake was right. After all, she wasn't operating at one hundred percent. She was barely even able to walk on her own. She probably didn't realize how bad off she still was. And he had said that the doctor had warned that she shouldn't over—

overex—overexer—oh, hell. She couldn't even come up with the word. She shouldn't overdo it.

She felt ridiculous. Jake was right. She needed her rest and here she was, pitching a fit about sex.

Skye managed to get the robe off and get underneath the covers. From now on, she'd listen better when he told her something. Of course he only had her best interests at heart.

She yawned, sinking down into the soft bed. The sheets were flannel, so much softer than the scratchy things she'd laid on in the hospital. As much as she wanted to be awake, she couldn't push back against the exhaustion.

Tomorrow, she'd apologize for being petulant. That'd smooth everything over.

But for now, she'd just look forward to waking up in Jake's arms.

Finally, he couldn't stall any longer. Jake had contacted his office assistant and read her the riot act about not forwarding calls from Keaton about this whole mess. He'd replied to emails, one from an oil company in Saudi Arabia about a three-month job and one from a company that was trying to get approval to run a pipeline from Alaska to Louisiana. That was a yearlong gig, but it was in North America. It'd be easier to travel and still see Grace.

He'd even gone down to the little home gym and run at a punishing speed on the treadmill, hoping to burn off the excess energy that Skye seemed to have inspired in him.

Now he was sweaty and hopefully not appealing in any sense. He had on the ratty pair of sweatshorts he slept in and an old T-shirt he'd gotten for free in college. Nothing "hot" there.

It was close to eleven when he silently slipped into the bedroom. It was dark and Skye didn't move on her side of the bed. Good.

He managed to avoid stubbing his toe on the dresser as he worked his way to the bed. But the bed shifted when he sat down and he saw how the covers had gotten tangled up around Skye.

Dang it, it was cold enough in the room that he was going to freeze to death without at least a corner of the blanket. He managed to wrestle a part of it away from her. He thought for a second that he'd managed to do so without disturbing Skye, but then she rolled over and curled up against him.

Oh, *hell*. She wasn't wearing anything. Not even the robe.

He didn't know where to put his hand. Wrapping his arm around her waist would put him too close to her bottom. But bending his arm at the elbow caused physical pain. He settled for stretching his arm out as far as possible along the bed.

"Hmm?" she hummed sleepily.

"It's okay," he told her, praying she wouldn't wake up anymore. "I'm here now."

"Mmm. Love you," she mumbled in reply. And then he felt her body relax into a deeper sleep.

It was hard *not* to feel it, frankly. She had one knee bent so that it overlapped his thigh and her small breasts were pressed against his chest—not to mention the tight hold she had on his waist. He was trapped under her body. It was not the place he wanted to be.

Jake lay there, repeatedly running through the very good reasons why he was gripping the bedsheets with enough force to tear them into strips. She was mentally compromised. She didn't remember that she wanted a divorce. She had forgotten that she didn't love him anymore.

But as the minutes ticked by into hours and

the sleep deprivation began to mess with him, he wondered if she would get those two terrible years back at all. Maybe the drifting apart, the fights—the big fight—would all be gone for good.

Maybe…maybe she would love him again. They could just go back to where they'd been before it all fell apart on them. He knew they couldn't really do that—they had a daughter now. No matter what form the future took, Grace would have to be a top priority. But…

What if Skye fell in love with him all over again?

God, his head was a mess—and he wasn't even the one who'd smacked it in a car wreck, for crying out loud. Would it even *be* possible to go back—hit the do-over button and begin again?

As she slept in his arms, he thought and thought and *thought*. Could she still love him?

Could he still love her?

Well, he knew the answer to that question. Of course he still loved her. Even as their marriage had unraveled, he'd loved her. He always had. He'd never stopped.

He just… Hell. He just hadn't done a great job of living with her.

Not that he was doing a great job of living with her right now, either. Of course she didn't remember him going to live in a hotel for a week before he flew over to Bahrain. He'd made sure the rent was covered for the year he was gone on the off chance they would decide to give it another try. He earned twenty times what Skye did with her graphic design business, after all. He wasn't looking to punish her. He just hadn't known if they could be together anymore.

Ten stinking months had passed and he was no closer to that answer. In fact, given the way she was sleeping on him, he'd say he was even further from a definitive answer than he'd been this morning.

If he could do it all over again, would he?

He lifted his arm and settled it around her bare waist.

He would. Heaven help him, he would.

Man, he was so screwed.

When Jake emerged into consciousness the next day, a couple of things hit him all at once. The combination was better than any coffee jolt. He went from zero to one hundred in three blinks of the eye.

Skye was rubbing his chest in long, even strokes.

Her hips were slowly tilting forward and back against his hip.

And he had a raging hard-on.

When he jolted into awareness, she murmured, "Good morning." Then her hand began to slip lower.

"Um, hey," he said, grabbing her hand before she could grab anything else. "Morning. You want some coffee? I'll go make coffee." He tried to peel her off of him, but for a petite woman, she was surprisingly good at anchoring him to the bed.

"I don't want coffee," she all but purred as she tested the grip he had on her hand. "I want you."

"How did you sleep?" he blurted out, desperate to avoid telling her *no* and equally desperate to avoid telling her *yes*. Blood began to pound in his ears, although he wasn't sure how much of it was panic and how much of it was lust.

"Wonderfully." And this time, she did purr as her hips flexed again. "I love waking up with you."

She had, once. Morning sex was the bonus of

being married. So was afternoon sex. And evening sex.

His body surged up—and up—at the memories. No. No! He was not going to give in. He was stronger than this.

"We should—we should probably, uh, do the physical therapy exercises first thing," he sputtered. Anything to avoid upsetting her—or taking advantage of her. "Doctor's orders."

In the grand scheme of things, it wasn't much of a lie. The doctor had, in fact, told Jake to make sure she did her exercises and stretches. Just not at—he turned his head and found a clock—8:43 in the morning. Crap. Maybe the doctor had. He must still be trying to adjust to central time after all those months in Bahrain.

"Can't it wait?" she asked as she kissed his shoulder. Then she skimmed her teeth over his skin.

"Nope." He yelped in surprise as desire hammered at a few very specific areas of his anatomy.

"Doesn't sex with my husband count as physical therapy?" At least she didn't sound upset—not yet, anyway. She was still trying her level best to seduce him.

And she was doing a pretty damn good job at the moment. Every fiber of his being wanted to roll into her and feel her move underneath him. He knew what she liked—it'd be easy to pin her hands over her head and drive in hard until their bodies surrendered to each other.

And, his traitorous mind unhelpfully pointed out, it'd erase the lackluster memory of their last lackluster sex.

The time when he'd accidentally gotten her pregnant.

Damn.

"Skye, baby," he pleaded as she nibbled her way up his shoulder and toward his neck. "Please. I don't have any condoms and you haven't been exactly on the pill recently. If I got you pregnant right now, that doctor of yours would probably have me arrested."

That worked. She stopped nibbling and tilting and trying to get her hand free of his grip. "Oh." The disappointment was obvious.

In his relief that he'd found an argument that she would buy, he made a fatal mistake. He loosened his grip on her hand.

She knew it, too. Before he could respond, she'd

wiggled her hand out of his and slid it down his shorts. Then she wrapped her fingers around his erection. "Other ways to have fun," she said, sliding her hand up and then down his length.

"Skye!"

"Don't be so shocked," she scolded him. "We used to fool around like this all the time, remember?"

Man, how could he forget? No man forgot the first time someone else's hand brought him to climax. It just didn't happen.

He wasn't going to make it. He was going to lose it and ravish her and hate himself the moment they were done because—

Suddenly, from somewhere far away, a bell rang. The doorbell.

Jake didn't know whether to laugh or cry. And he didn't stop to think about it. He pried her hand off of him and all but threw himself out of the bed. "I'll get it. And start that coffee. And then we'll do the prescribed exercises."

He didn't know if she was upset or disappointed or what. He didn't stick around long enough to gauge her reaction. Instead—and he was not proud of this—he bolted from the room and raced down the stairs. As he flung the door open, he realized he'd been saved by the bell. The thought made him laugh.

"Morning?" Whit Daltry gave Jake a confused look when he opened the door. "Everything okay?"

"What?" Jake realized he must be quite the sight—bed head and yesterday's workout clothes and laughing his fool head off. "Oh, yeah. Everything's fine. Skye just told a joke, that's all."

Then Whit turned and Jake realized the man wasn't alone. "Jake, this is my fiancée, Megan."

"Ma'am," Jake said, shaking her hand as well.

"It's so nice to finally meet you," Megan said. She opened her mouth to say something else, but then took in his appearance and seemed to think better of it. "We're sorry to wake you," she said tactfully. "But we wanted to see if there was anything we could do for you and Skye."

Yeah, Jake could guess what she was thinking. Megan had probably heard a whole truckload of gossip by now. Four years' worth. He cleared his throat and willed his anatomy to stand down, for God's sake. "Come in. Skye's not up yet—we were just about to do her PT."

"We won't keep you from your therapy…" Whit began.

"No—it's fine. Come in. I insist!" Because if he could get Whit and Megan to hang out for a while, then Skye wouldn't be able to pick up where she'd left off. He wracked his brain for something that would convince the two of them to stay. "It's—uh—it's a beautiful home. And Skye really loves how you decorated the bedroom."

"Thanks," Whit said as he continued to stare at Jake as if he had boiled lobsters crawling out of his ears. "We usually rent this to oil executives who are in town for more than a few days."

Jake backed up a step, hoping to get Whit and Megan to follow him in. They didn't. "Well, it's just wonderful. Megan!" he said a little too loudly as another bolt of inspiration struck him. Megan jolted in surprise and stepped to the side, so that she was half hidden behind Whit. Aw, crap—Jake wasn't making the best of impressions here, but desperate times called for desperate measures. "Skye's going to need some clothes and necessities. I'm going to try and hire someone to bring the rest of our stuff from Houston. But that's going to take a few days. Where's a good place to pick up a couple of outfits?"

"I can get her a few things. Do you know her size?"

"Uh…" He didn't want to go check because that meant he'd have to go back into the bedroom where Skye was probably still naked. "Small, probably. Most of her things were lost in the storm."

Megan and Whit shared a look. *Hell.* Jake could just imagine what the gossip was. No, actually—wait. He couldn't. And he didn't want to. He and Skye had probably been the hot topic of gossips on and off ever since they'd slipped away the night after the very public fight with their parents. People would believe whatever they wanted to.

Whit nodded. "Big city, Houston. Nothing like Royal. We're just up the road, so if you need anything, you give us a call," he added. "We've sure been worried about Skye for these past few months."

"I'll pick her up a couple of outfits," Megan added, backing away slowly. "Lounge pants and the like. Good for doing therapy in."

Crap, they were leaving. "Are you sure you can't stay?"

"We really must be going," Megan said. "But it's been nice to meet you. I'll drop off a few things for Skye."

"Jake," Whit said with a nod of his head.

"Thanks," Jake said, resigned to the fact that this distraction had been temporary. Maybe when Megan brought by the clothes, she and Skye would start chatting. Yeah, that'd be good—some quality girl time to divert her attention from sex.

He shut the door and then, just because he needed to have some sense knocked into him, he banged his head against the wood a few times.

"Who was it?"

At the sound of Skye's voice, Jake whirled around. She'd made it halfway down the steps and was leaning heavily on the railing.

She was wearing the T-shirt and pants she'd come home in, but she looked a million times better than she had yesterday. There was a brightness about her that made him want to stare. Aside from the haircut, she was the woman he'd loved *so* much.

"Whit Daltry and his fiancée, Megan," Jake explained, trying to find somewhere else to look and not doing an awesome job of it.

"What did they want?" She took another cautious step downward.

"To see how you were doing. Megan offered to pick you up some clothes." He considered his options. The good news was that she was dressed and out of the bed.

How much longer was he going to be able to keep this up?

"Well, you're almost down here. Might as well see how you take the rest of those steps and then I'll get the coffee."

He climbed up the last few steps and took her arm—if he had a grip on her, she couldn't grab him. Then they made it down the rest of the way.

"Whew," Skye said. "That's hard work." She tried to give him a jokey smile, but she couldn't quite pull it off.

"This is why we have to do the exercises first," he explained as he led her to the couch. Once he had her sitting down—and the recliner reclining—he said, "It's going to take a while before you're back up to full strength. If you overexert yourself, it's going to knock you down."

"Overexert! That's the word I couldn't remember." She grinned up at him, but then her face darkened. "I'm sorry, Jake. I should have listened to you. I know I can't do everything all at once."

That was all it took to make him feel like a jerk. "It's okay, babe. I can see how you want to make up for lost time."

A smile lit up her face. "I just don't want to miss another second with you."

His heart about stopped. He wanted to tell her the truth. He needed to—this wasn't just a matter of self-preservation, but of honor. He felt wrong letting her go on under the delusion that they were still a happy couple.

"Skye…"

"Yes?" She looked up at him with her big blue eyes. She'd always been his blue-eyed Skye. Always.

And the doctor had said not to tell her the truth. It would upset her and that would be a setback. And the more setbacks she had, the longer Jake would be trapped in this godforsaken town.

"I'm—I'm really impressed you made it downstairs on your own."

"Thanks, hon." But the trip had clearly taken a

lot out of her. She leaned back in the recliner and closed her eyes. She looked younger right then, more like the woman he'd run away with and less the like woman he'd left behind. "I believe someone's been trying to make me coffee since I woke up?"

"Right," he said, thankful for the concrete task. "Then we'll do the exercises."

"Can't wait," he heard her groan as he headed to the kitchen to figure out the coffeemaker.

He laughed.

It was a good feeling.

# Five

Jake brought her coffee and a bowl of cereal. "After we do your exercises, I'll run out to the store and get some of the things you like," he said when she scowled at the boring bowl of flakes. "We can't survive on delivery pizza, after all."

"I would kill for a croissant," she admitted.

She ate her cereal. Suddenly, she was not looking forward to the exercises. Her mind still thought she was in shape—but Jake was right. The trip downstairs had taken a lot out of her. Stupid legs and their stupid muscles.

Still, the coffee was good and the cereal was... filling.

Jake took her dishes and then came back into the

room. He helped her stand and then he was lowering her to the ground. "On your back," he said.

She did as he said, but she waggled her eyebrows at him. "I thought you'd never ask."

He grinned at her, but it seemed...forced somehow. "Okay," he said, looking at a pile of papers on the coffee table. "Let's start with leg lifts. Doesn't that sound awesome?"

She gave him a look. "Not unless you're suddenly defining *awesome* in a new and unpleasant way."

Jake watched her lying there for a moment. "Aren't you going to start?"

"Start what? There are a bunch of different leg lifts. Straight leg? Bent leg?" Heck, even all this talking was wearing her down. "I can't see the picture, you know."

"Oh. Sorry." He held the paper in front of her face. Ah. Bent leg lifts. "It says to keep your feet flat on the floor and extend your leg until it's straight for ten reps, then do the other side."

"Wonderful," she grunted in an entirely unsexy way as she tried to get her legs to bend. "A little help here?"

Jake paused again, and then helped her bend her legs. "Right first," he said. "I'll count."

Skye managed to do a whole three leg lifts before she ran out of steam. "Can I quit now?"

He wrinkled his nose at her. "Seven more. Move that leg, Skye."

"You're going to have to help me," she informed him. Her leg was already shaking from the effort. "I can't do this."

"Yes, you can." Then, after another moment's hesitation, he put his hands on her calf. "Slow and steady wins the race."

Despite the sweat that was beginning to bead on her forehead, she grinned. This was not one of their sexier touches, but even just his hand on her leg was enough to make her more…energetic.

They managed to make it through the rest of the set until Jake finally guided her foot back to the floor. By this time she was panting. "I'm gonna need a reward after this," she told him.

He froze. "I can get you some ice cream. You probably shouldn't have wine just yet."

"That's not the reward I was thinking of," she grumbled as he helped her do the next set of lifts.

"I'm just trying to get you better," he quickly defended.

"Hmph," she replied, but then the lifts got harder and harder and it took all of her concentration to make it through the last few. "Are we done now?"

"You're cute," he said in an offhand way as he flipped to another page. "Here—this one is in the same position."

"Oh, joy."

"Pelvic tilts." He held the picture in front of her. "Set of ten reps. It says…" She saw him swallow. "Lift your bottom off the ground and squeeze your muscles. Hold for five seconds. This one's for your abs and glutes."

"And *then* we're done?"

"Nope. Then we get to do stomach exercises." He had the nerve to sound happy about this.

"Better be a damn good reward." She tried lifting her bottom up, but she couldn't hold it for a count of five.

Jake sighed wearily and then slid his hand underneath to help hold her up. "Focus on squeezing your muscles."

"I hate you right now. You know that, right?"

He didn't reply.

After the pelvic tilts, he helped her roll over and then helped her lift her leg straight toward the ceiling. If she'd thought the stupid leg lifts were hard before, these lifts left her so drained that she couldn't even complain about them.

Then, halfway through the second set, a muscle cramp hit her with the force of a sledgehammer to the butt. "Ow. Ow ow ow *ow*! Cramp!"

"Where?" he demanded, sounding as panicked as she felt.

"Here. *Here*! OW!" She managed to get her hand up to point to the cheek in question.

Then he put his hands on her bottom and began to rub. "Does this help? Because if it doesn't, I'll stop."

"More!" she shouted.

So he kept going. He kneaded her muscle until the cramp had passed. "Better?" he asked.

Well, she was. But she wasn't in the mood to tell him that just yet. "Just a little longer," she said. Now that the sharpness of the cramp had faded, she had to admit the massage was nice. More than nice. "I don't know how much more I can do." That was the truth, too. She didn't want to cramp up anymore.

Then Jake's hands left her body. The loss of his touch and heat made her want to whimper. "Let's see… We're supposed to do two more on the floor, but they're stretches. Damn."

"What?"

"Nothing," he hurried to say. "I just have to stretch your legs. Roll back over."

Skye managed to do that. Then Jake picked up her leg. "Keep the other one straight," he said, studying the picture. "And keep this foot flexed."

Skye did as he told her to as he lifted her leg so it was perpendicular to her body. The tension was tight in the back of her legs. "Feeling that?" he asked

"Oh, yeah." He was standing between her legs, his hands on her body. What she wouldn't give to not be wearing these ugly clothes. And she hated that she was too weak to do much of anything but let him stretch her muscles.

They did the one leg, then the other. Another cramp hit her, this time in the calf. "Ow!"

"Here?" he said, going right for the sore muscle.

"Ah, that's it." She sighed in relief as he worked the tension out of her body.

"I'll call Lark later, ask what we can do to avoid

the cramps," he said, not looking at Skye as he massaged her body.

She managed to get her hands up and get hold of his shirt. "Thank you, babe," she murmured, trying to pull him down into her. She might not be able to do anything that was terribly energetic right now, but she could still properly kiss him.

"What are you doing?" he asked, looking alarmed.

"Kissing you," she replied. "I want something to make all that worthwhile."

For a moment, she wasn't sure he was going to let her kiss him—but she didn't understand why. Why was he pushing back against sex so hard?

"Just a kiss," he murmured, looking at her lips. "One kiss. As your reward." Then he put his arms on either side of her head and leaned down into her.

Oh, how she had dreamed of this—feeling his weight surround her.

"I…I missed you, Skye." He said it as if he couldn't believe it. "I missed this."

"Me, too, babe."

He lowered his lips to hers. At first, it seemed as if he was just going to give her a chaste little peck. *Oh, no,* she thought as she ran her fingers into his hair. Now that she finally had him, she wasn't about to settle for a half kiss. It was all or nothing.

"Skye," he groaned into her as she ran her tongue over his lips. "Oh, babe."

And then? *Then* he kissed her. He kissed her *hard*, taking everything she offered. If he'd kissed her like this before the exercises, she would have had more to give him. As it was, she was barely able to loop her legs over his, damn it.

Not that he needed any help. He thrust against her, with only the ugly pants standing between them. *"Oh,"* she moaned into his mouth. "Oh, *Jake.*"

She shouldn't have done that because he stopped thrusting against her and kissing her. "Sorry," he mumbled as he pushed himself off of her. "Didn't mean to let it go that long."

She stared at him in confusion as he stood. "You didn't?" She managed to prop herself up into a sitting position—she wasn't going to let him get away from her, not this time—but when she tried to stand, her legs went all gelatin on her. "Oops!"

So she couldn't chase him down. But failing to

stand on her own worked as a way to lure him back, too. He was by her side in an instant, lifting her up and setting her back onto the couch. "Easy, babe," he said. His voice was gentle, but his face? It was dark and pissed-looking. "You're overdoing it again. You need to recover before you try anything else. I'll get you something to drink."

"I'm not done with you yet," she called after him. She wanted another kiss—and a whole lot more. She wanted to be sweaty and naked beneath him, their bodies joined together in every way she could physically manage and a few she probably couldn't.

He paused in the doorway to the kitchen and turned back to look at her. "Are you sure?"

"Of course I'm sure. You can't kiss me like that and expect me not to want to seduce you."

He gave her a tight little smile that didn't look happy. "I won't," he promised her. "I won't."

*I. Can. Not. Sleep. With. Skye.*

And he was going to keep repeating that particular statement until he got it through his thick skull.

But dammit…when she'd been mouthing off to

him during PT and then so desperate for a kiss—well, maybe he wasn't as strong a man as he liked to think.

Because right now, she was acting exactly like the woman he'd loved his whole life. Sassy and sultry and ready to challenge him at the drop of a hat.

He knew darned well and good that, if she could, she'd chase him down and refuse to settle for just a kiss.

What was he going to do? He hadn't even been alone in the house with her for twenty-four hours yet and her recovery was going to take weeks—months, even. Months of fending off her advances—of trying to find a way to do so without upsetting her. How long before she remembered that she'd wanted a divorce? How long would he have to play the part of the doting husband? How damn long would he have to lie in bed with her and not make love to her?

Plus, there were also the logistics of the situation. Yeah, he could afford to pass on the next job—but how long could he do that before his company's reputation took a hit? That was no small thing. Yes, he was a millionaire—but he worked for his fortune. He couldn't retire, not yet.

And then there was the fact that he was, at this very moment, living in Royal, Texas. He'd vowed never to come back here and yet, here he was.

He'd run into Keaton within fifteen minutes of crossing city limits. How much longer could he possibly avoid his parents—or worse, Skye's parents? He did not want to deal with Gloria and David Holt, even if Keaton and Lark said they were nicer humans now. And Jake especially did not want to deal with Vera and Tyrone Taylor.

But…he was stuck. Hell, at this point, he didn't even feel all that good about leaving Skye alone so he could run to the store and grab some real food. What if she got it in her head to try the stairs on her own and, after this round of exercises, failed to make it?

Horrible images of her lying broken on the stairs, her head bleeding from where she'd hit it on the railing or wall, crowded into his mind.

Damn it all. He needed help and he couldn't ask Lark and Keaton to ride to his rescue again. They had his daughter. That was more than he should even have to ask of them. But he needed *someone*.

His stomach lurching, he picked up his phone and dialed the old number from memory. Funny how easily it came back to him after all this time.

"Hello?"

*Mom.* For a second, he almost hung up. The last time they'd spoken, on that horrible night when everything had come to a head, she'd been more concerned with backing up his father than understanding how much Skye meant to him. He'd vowed never to speak to his parents again. But Lark and Keaton had said they'd changed.

"Hi, Mom. It's me—" He didn't get anything else out.

His mother made a little strangled noise and said, "Jake? Jake, honey, is that you?"

"Yeah." He swallowed. He was doing this for Skye and for Grace. Not for himself. "It's me."

"Keaton said you were here, but I was afraid to get my hopes up—oh, honey." She made a noise that sounded like a sniff.

*Oh, God—don't cry.* He couldn't deal with that

right now. "Yeah. I'm back in town. Looks like I'm going to be staying for a little while."

There was a weird click on the other end of the line. "Jake." He started at the gruff sound of David Holt's voice. Lord, Jake was barely prepared to talk to his mother, but his father, too? This was rapidly going from bad to worse. "Where are you at?"

Still, he'd made this call. He had to plow through, no matter how much he wanted to hang up. "Skye's with me. I got us a place in Pine Valley."

"Have you seen Grace?" his mother asked.

"Yeah. Yesterday. I don't know if Skye is strong enough to go see her today, but I'm hoping to take her tomorrow."

"Did you two get married?" his father demanded.

Jake gritted his teeth. "Yes. Three days after we left." He waited for—well, he didn't know what. The parents he knew would start reading him the riot act about throwing his lot in with a lying, cheating Taylor.

"Good," his father said. "You should have."

"Well, I did." He tried not to snarl it, but he wasn't sure he succeeded.

His mother made a tired noise. "How's Skye today? Is she all right?"

"Fine. We just did her exercises and she's resting."

"We've prayed so hard for her—for both of you," his mother said.

"You *did*?" That didn't mesh with the way he remembered his parents issuing that final ultimatum that he stop running around with Skye and start acting like a real Holt—more like Keaton.

"Oh, honey, I know things ended badly—" his father made a *harrumphing* noise "—but we're just so glad you're okay and Skye is getting better. Is there anything we can do to help?"

Jake actually pulled the phone away from his ear and stared at it. Maybe these weren't his parents. Maybe they'd been replaced by space aliens or something.

Keaton and Lark had said that Gloria and David Holt had changed. But never in his wildest dreams had Jake figured they would have changed *this* much. "You're not mad at me? At Skye?"

There was a pause on the other end of the line. Jake realized he was holding his breath. "What good's it going to do?" his mother finally said. "It would just drive you and Skye away again—and this time you'll take Grace with you."

"She's a sweetie," his father added, sounding thoughtful.

"Now," his mother went on in a businesslike tone, "you tell us what you need."

He didn't know what else to say at this point. *I'm not sorry I left? I'm not happy about being back?* Yeah, that didn't seem like the way to go.

"Well, groceries, I guess. Skye's still pretty weak. I'm afraid to leave her alone, but there's not much to eat in this house."

"Of course. I was going to run errands this afternoon anyway. I'll pick up some of your favorite things and, oh! I'll bring a dish," Gloria said, which made Jake smile. That, at least, hadn't changed. "Jake," she added, and he heard her voice waver. Was she crying? "Honey, we're glad you're back."

"We sure are," David said. He didn't sound happy, but then, Jake's dad wasn't the most expressive of guys.

The fact that he was even admitting out loud that he was happy Jake was here was...well, it was something. What, Jake wasn't sure, but it was *something*.

"Yeah, okay," Jake said. He gave them the address and added, "See you soon." He hung up.

He stared at his phone, feeling a weird time/space disconnect. He almost dialed the Taylor number, but then he remembered the look on Lark's face when he'd asked if her parents had been by to see the baby.

One set of parents at a time. And right now, his parents were the safest bet. Jake could deal with the Taylors later. Plus, if his parents were in the house, Skye couldn't try to seduce him again. So that counted for…something.

He sighed. No matter how he dressed it up, he was not looking forward to this. "Babe?" he said, going back into the living room.

"Hmm?" She blinked at him sleepily. "Were you on the phone?"

"Yeah. I called my parents." Or, at the very least, he'd called people who sounded like his parents.

Her eyes opened wider. "And?"

He didn't want to upset her, so he stuck to the facts. "They're going to pick up some groceries so I won't have to leave you alone."

"They…are?" She looked confused, which Jake

supposed wasn't weird—he was still pretty con-fused by the whole conversation himself.

"Yeah. Mom's bringing a dish. They seemed ex-cited to see us." He made sure to emphasize the "us" so that Skye would know she was included in that.

"But I—I look terrible!" Her brow wrinkled. "Oh, man—I'm still wearing the same clothes as yesterday."

He grinned. Of all the things to worry about, that was really pretty low on the list. "You look fine. And remember how I said Megan was going to pick up a few things for you?"

She sat back in the chair and he could tell she was thinking—hard. "Oh. Okay. I remember that."

"Good, babe. You just rest, okay? I'm going to go take a quick shower." He wasn't exactly vain, but yeah—first time he saw his parents in four years? He wanted to be dressed a little better than his workout gear.

She sank back into the chair and let her eyes drift closed again. "Maybe tomorrow we can shower together."

He froze. What was he supposed to say to that?

He'd barely kept it together when she'd been in the tub and he'd been fully dressed. How was he going to keep his hands off of her if they were *both* wet and naked?

# Six

Skye was working up the energy to kiss Jake again. She'd been sitting on the couch for a while, watching game shows and dozing, and she was pretty sure she'd recovered from the stretching enough that she could get to her feet and walk over to where Jake was sitting at the table, working on his computer.

She didn't like that. Something in her mind wanted to complain about the amount of time he worked—but that also felt foolish. After all, he'd only logged a couple of hours last night. And he'd only been sitting over there for about thirty minutes this morning, after he'd showered and shaved and come back downstairs looking more handsome in a pair of jeans and a light blue button-up shirt than she remembered.

So it wasn't as if he was ignoring her or anything. He *had* to work—she was only starting to think about what the hospital bills were going to look like and she had no idea where she was with any of her clients. She could only hope they'd found other graphic designers to finish their projects.

But that kiss earlier…*wow*. That was the kind of kiss a woman dreamed about. For a blindingly clear moment, she hadn't felt weak or tired or confused. She'd been the woman she'd been before the accident—claimed by a single kiss from Jake Holt.

She needed more. One was not enough. It never had been.

She managed to get the footrest down on the recliner and her bottom scooted to the edge of the seat when the doorbell rang again. She shot the door a dirty look. Who were all these people and why were they constantly foiling her plans to seduce her husband?

"I've got it," he said as he shot her a wry smile. "Don't get up."

It'd taken too much effort to get the footrest down. She wasn't going to put it back up. Instead, she sat, listening.

"Oh, hi—that's great. Come on in." Jake led a curvaceous, beautiful redhead into the room.

Jealousy gripped Skye, which was ridiculous because she didn't even know who this woman was. But she was beautiful and Skye couldn't help but envy her curves. Skye looked down at her small breasts and not-there hips that were hidden under baggy, unisex clothes, and remembered her own half-and-half haircut. Ugh. No wonder Jake wasn't interested.

"Skye, this is Megan Maguire—she's engaged to Whit Daltry, the man we're renting the house from."

She was not in the mood for visitors. She just wasn't. "Hi."

"It's so good to meet you, Skye," Megan gushed. "We're all just so glad you're awake! You were quite the story."

Jake cleared his throat and shot what looked like a meaningful gaze at Megan. But then he looked back at Skye. "Megan stopped by this morning—

remember? I told you that she was going to pick up some new clothes for you."

"Jake said you were a small—I hope that's right," Megan said with a wide grin.

Skye cringed. Her mother had always picked out clothes for her—dressing Skye as though she were a mini-Vera Taylor in frilly dresses and white pants that wrinkled and stained if Skye looked at them wrong.

In Houston, Skye had favored simple clothes— blue jeans and yoga pants, with light cotton tops. She'd had a couple of sexy dresses for when she and Jake were able to afford a night out.

Megan held up a big shopping bag. Yes, Skye did remember Jake saying something about Megan bringing clothes for…oh! Because his parents were coming over and if she remembered anything, it was that she was always trying to win over Gloria and David Holt—or, at the very least, Gloria.

Things had changed and she had a second chance to make a first impression. Skye forced herself to smile. God only knew what was in that bag, but it couldn't be worse than what she had on now. "Yeah, I'm a small." She eyed Megan's figure and wondered what kind of clothes this woman had picked out—certainly not the sort of thing that would fit Skye's flat chest.

She shouldn't be jealous. She knew this was an overreaction. Jake had always reassured her that he loved her body just the way it was.

Megan looked her over. "I grabbed a few other necessities. Would you like me to brush your hair out?"

Skye touched the side of her head. "Would you? It's still kind of hard to lift my arms at this point."

"Sure can." Megan beamed.

"There's a bathroom down here," Jake said, looking relieved. "I've got some work to do. Megan, thanks so much," he added.

He helped Skye to her feet and then led her to the bathroom. Done in creams and reds, it was lovely, much like the rest of the house. "I'll leave you ladies to it," he said as he escaped.

"All right," Megan said gleefully before turning to Skye. "First order of business—we've got to get you out of those hideous clothes. No offense."

"None taken. Thanks for doing this for me. I don't even know you."

"I manage the Royal Safe Haven animal shelter," Megan explained as she unpacked the bag she'd been carrying. It contained a brush, hair bands, deodorant and a small makeup palette with a pink lipstick, a nearly matching pink blush and three shades of eye shadow. "I thought you might want to feel pretty after being in a hospital for so long," she explained.

Skye gaped at the goodies. Never had pink lipstick looked *so* good. "How did you know?"

"You've been in that bed for a long time and I've got eyes," Megan told her as she laid out three pairs of yoga pants—black, gray and navy—and some really cute tops. "That Jake Holt is a fine specimen. I just figured that any woman would want to look her best for him." She held up a six-pack of bikini briefs. "Will these work?"

Skye nodded. They were the right size and in bright patterns. Sure, cotton underwear wasn't silk and lace, but she could envision how parading around in nothing but a tiny pair of panties would be sure to get Jake's attention. "Perfect."

"Which top do you want right now?"

"That one," Skye said, pointing to the one that was a robin's-egg blue with a white trim.

"I thought so."

Megan helped Skye get her T-shirt off and the new top over her head without commenting on Skye's underwhelming assets. Then she got the brush. "Any spot I should avoid?"

Skye showed her where the hair was shorter. "It's still a little sore," she explained.

"Very punk," Megan said approvingly. "Although if you wanted to experiment, a pixie cut would look fabulous on you."

"I've never had it short," Skye said as Megan brushed her hair. "I don't even know what that would look like."

"No worries, then. How about a low ponytail pulled to the side?"

"You're good at this," Skye told her as Megan began to create order out of the chaos that was her head.

"Dog grooming," Megan laughed as she twisted in the hair band. "Okay, let me see your face."

In short order, Skye had shadow on her lids, a little blush on her cheeks and a touch of color on her lips. "He always was a fine specimen," Skye said as Megan applied the finishing touches. She didn't know why she was opening up to this woman, but she felt as if she needed to explain.

"We've been together since I was six and he was seven."

Megan whistled. "That long?"

"He's always been the one," Skye told her. "Always."

"Then you'll look your best for him." Megan helped Skye stand.

Skye looked at her reflection. The side ponytail managed to hide the shorter hair. The makeup was subtle, but the color on her cheeks and the shade of the shirt made her eyes pop. "Wow, I look *normal*."

"Is that good?"

Skye snorted. "Compared to where I was? This is *fabulous*." Sure, she wasn't dressed for a hot night out on the town, but just to be wearing a top that fit her was such a vast improvement. "You think Jake will like it?"

"I think he'll have a hard time keeping his hands off of you," Megan said with a wink.

"Mission accomplished!" Skye replied. She pivoted. She still had on the baggy pants, but the top was fitted with darts at the waist. She looked like a woman again. "It's wonderful. I can't thank you enough, Megan."

"Don't mention it," Megan said. "We all had to pull together after that storm. You have Jake give me a call if you need something else."

"I will." Skye hugged Megan. This—this was something she'd wanted. She and Jake had been on their own for so long, with no one else who'd come to their aid when they needed it. Skye had wanted to return to Royal because she'd missed the community—even something as simple as a neighbor who was good at dog grooming. "Come visit again," she told Megan. "And when I'm stronger, we'll have to go out for coffee or something."

Megan gave her a sly smile. "Oh, I have a feeling I'll be seeing you again before too much longer. I'll leave you to that fine specimen of yours."

After Megan left the bathroom, Skye managed to get the baggy pants off and, leaning heavily on the counter, put a cute pair of pink and white panties and the new gray yoga pants on. It was only when she was pulling everything up that she noticed her stomach—and the long red scar that cut across the lower part.

*That's right*, she thought, tracing the scar with her fingertips. *I had a baby. Grace.*

Longing filled her. She'd wanted a child so

badly, but they'd been waiting until their finances were a little more stable.

And somehow…she'd had Grace. She didn't remember even being pregnant. She hated that. She should remember being pregnant. But it just wasn't there.

She found herself staring at her hand. She didn't have her ring on—she didn't have her earrings in, either. Maybe Lark had them? If they hadn't been lost in the wreck? She couldn't remember.

Suddenly, she wanted that ring and those earrings back. Jake had gotten them for her…had that been last year? Yes, that seemed about right. He'd gotten her very expensive diamonds because—because—damn it. Because he could afford them, he'd said. To make up for the small wedding ring. Was that right?

Skye wanted to thump the side of her own head to try and jar some of the memories loose from the holes they were all stuck in.

She wouldn't have lost the earrings in the tornado, would she? She studied her earlobes. The diamonds had had screw backs, she remembered. It'd taken her almost ten minutes to get them in properly when Jake had given them to her on…on their anniversary. Yes, that felt right. And she'd just left them in. It was too hard to take out every night. She'd gotten used to them being there, as if they were a part of her. Just like the ring was.

The screws wouldn't have come unscrewed, would they? Those were serious earrings. And her lobes hadn't been torn through, she saw. So the earrings were…where?

She wanted them back. Jake had bought them for her.

She would not panic. She just had to remember to ask her sister if the hospital had given her the ring and earrings. Those were things Jake had given her. She hoped she hadn't lost them.

After a final check of her reflection, she decided she'd ask Jake to take her to see her daughter soon.

But the first order of business was to show Jake the new and improved her.

Jake tried to focus on his work. He had several emails from his contacts in Bahrain that required his full attention. The system he'd helped install had experienced a few hiccups since his departure and he really, *really* didn't want to have to fly back over to the Middle East at this point.

Ah, good. The North American job he'd bid on wanted to schedule a video interview to discuss what Texas Sky Technologies could do for their project and they were flexible on the start date. If Jake wanted to take two weeks of the vacation time at the beginning of the contract, he could.

That was good. He'd sent back some times he hoped he'd be available for the interview and then considered the best way to go about making sure he was.

Maybe if the visit with his parents went well, they could come by again. Or Jake could take Skye to Lark's and let her play with the baby. There had to be a way to make it work.

That was a lot of ifs and he knew it.

He kept glancing back toward the small hall that led to the bathroom. How long had they been in there? Jake was afraid Megan would let something slip that would confuse Skye. And that would be bad.

It wasn't helping that his parents would be over soon. He was nervous. The last time he'd seen either of them was…that last night. Jake and Skye had been having a romantic dinner at Claire's, the nicest restaurant in this town. It'd been the anniversary of their first time together. For a couple as inseparable as Jake and Skye had been, there really wasn't a first-date anniversary or first-meeting anniversary. They'd always just been together. So they'd taken to celebrating their first time. Romantic dinner, candles, wine—the whole nine yards. Jake had been out of college for a year and Skye had just graduated. They'd been adults and had decided they could go public with their relationship.

In retrospect, it wasn't the smartest thing they'd ever done. The blowup had been epic. He and Skye had left the next night and he, at least, had never looked back.

That was all in the past now, he reminded himself. And he couldn't change the past.

"She'll be out in a minute," Megan said, sailing into the room. "I got her all fixed up." She handed Jake the receipt for the clothes.

"That's great." But even as he said it, he realized that might not be a good thing. He was already having enough trouble keeping his hands off of Skye in those hideous clothes. How hard would it be to steer clear of her when she looked good?

He dug out his wallet and handed Megan two fifties. "Really appreciate it."

"I'm happy to help. I tried not to say anything that might confuse her," she added. "I don't know if you realize it, but the whole town has been rooting for her to pull through. She's come to symbolize Royal. We're all just thrilled that she's on the road to recovery." Megan looked at her watch. "Oh, I've got to go—a transfer of kittens is coming in. You call me if you need anything else, okay?"

"Thanks," Jake said, showing her out. And he did appreciate it. But he still would feel weird about having to call someone for help—someone who wasn't Skye, that was.

Man, he was not used to this depending-on-other-people thing.

"Jake?" From behind, Skye's voice reached out and caressed him. "What do you think?"

He knew even before he turned around that he was in trouble. He could hear it in her voice—she knew she looked good.

*I. Can. Not. Sleep. With. Skye*, he repeated as he pivoted.

Even knowing that she was going to look better

didn't prepare him for what he saw. Megan had gotten her hair smooth and in a neat little ponytail. He couldn't even see the shorter hairs. The clothes were close-cut and flattered her slender figure. And…

And she was wearing makeup. Of course she was. Megan would have come prepared, damn it.

"Well?" She managed to do a little turn to show him how the tight pants cupped her bottom. His hands started to itch. Would it be so wrong to help himself to her body, instead of helping her through a rep?

*Yes.* Yes, it would. He ground his teeth together and forced his hands to stay at his sides as she finished her turn.

"You look amazing," he told her—and he was not glossing over the truth this time.

"I feel *so* much better," she told him. "I need to write Megan a thank-you note." Her brow wrinkled. "Can you remind me to do that?"

"Sure." Then, helpless, he watched her take hesitant strides to where he was standing. She wobbled a little, but she kept her balance and didn't collapse into his arms.

She was going to kiss him and, because he

wasn't looking at the Skye who'd served him with divorce papers—hadn't been talking to that Skye for the last day—he was going to let her. He was powerless to resist this Skye.

Her arms slid around his neck. Yes, she leaned into him a little more than she might normally, but she seemed so far from the woman he'd had to carry into the house yesterday that he couldn't mentally reconcile all the different versions of Skye in his mind.

As she pulled his head down to hers, all he could think was that this was *his* blue-eyed Skye. *His*.

He sagged back against the door as he surrendered to her kiss. The weight of her body against his took what control he had and smashed it to small, unrecognizable bits. He knew—*knew*—there were valid reasons why he shouldn't be kissing her, shouldn't be encouraging her to kiss him some more, but for the life of him, he couldn't remember what those reasons were.

Not when she nipped at his lower lip. Not when she opened her mouth for him. And not when she rubbed against him, her body setting his on fire.

He couldn't help it. His hands slid down her back until he was palming her bottom. Small and firm—just like she was—just enough to hold. Perfect for him. Perfect.

"Jake," she whispered as he directed his kisses lower—down her neck, toward her exposed collarbone. "Don't stop. Don't—"

The bell rang. Again.

This was getting to be a pattern.

They both jumped. "What is with that damned doorbell?" Skye demanded. Then she looked at him and smiled. "Lipstick. Pink is not entirely your shade."

The doorbell rang again. Jake scrubbed the back of his hand over his face and steadied Skye on her feet before he answered the door.

And there, on the stoop, stood his mother. She seemed smaller than he remembered, the lines on her face a little deeper.

"Jacob Holt! Oh, my baby…I can't believe you're here!"

Next to him, Skye gasped as Gloria Holt rushed into the house and swallowed Jake up in a massive mama-bear hug.

"Uh—hi, Mom," he said, struggling to breathe through the grip she had him in.

"And Skye!" Gloria released Jake and turned to

Skye, who looked like a deer caught in the head-lights.

The next thing either of them knew, Gloria had wrapped her arms around Skye. "My word, it's just so good to see you up and about. We've been worried sick about you, sweetie."

"You…have?" Skye asked.

"Easy, Mom," Jake said, trying to pry his mother off of his wife.

"Son," David Holt said, as he came through the door next, his arms full of paper grocery sacks. Which meant there wouldn't be any awkward hugging from the older man. At least, not yet.

"Dad," Jake said. "Let me help you out."

"I got it," his dad said gruffly. Yeah, some things hadn't changed. "Skye, it's good to see you up and around."

Skye gave David a worried smile. "It is?"

"Oh, dear, you don't remember, do you?" Gloria clucked. "You look so much better than you did in that hospital."

"You came to see me in the hospital?"

"Why, of course we did! I made it in two or three times a week to spend time with Grace and I'd come sit with you and read to you." Gloria looked wistful. "I've been praying for you to come back to us."

"You *have*?" This time, Skye was less worried and more confused.

*"Mom,"* Jake said with a warning in his voice. "We're taking it slow and easy here." Because this crash course in Holt reintroductions wasn't going down easy. Skye was beginning to look panicked. Since his dad wouldn't let him help with the groceries, Jake stepped back to wrap his arm protectively around her waist.

"Oh—yes. Of course. I'm sorry, sweetie."

"You read to me?"

"I'll just put these away," David said, neatly sidestepping a conversation that might contain emotions. *What a surprise*, thought Jake.

"I sure did." Gloria watched her husband until he was safely in the kitchen. "I know David isn't the best with expressing his feelings—"

Jake choked. Yeah, that was one way to put it.

"But," Gloria went on, "when they found you pregnant and they managed to save you and Grace—well, you gave us a granddaughter. We're family now, honey."

Then Gloria swallowed them both up in another monster hug. Jake was afraid she was crying.

"Anyway," Gloria said, stepping back and dabbing at her eyes, "when Jake called this morning, I jumped at the chance pick up some groceries. Honey, you just look wonderful. I'm so glad you're both here together."

"Mom," Jake said again, glaring at her. "Slow. Easy." *Stop talking before you screw something up*, he mentally added.

Because the last thing he needed was his parents to inadvertently set Skye off.

"Of course, dear," she said, patting his arm. "I brought a casserole—chicken enchiladas. Your favorite, Jake!"

"That sounds…good," Skye said, sounding a little better.

"I'll get the last bags," David Holt said as he passed by them. "Your mother bought enough to last you weeks."

Gloria was still standing there, beaming at the two of them. Well. Aside from his mother's habit of talking enough for both her and her husband, this actually wasn't bad. His parents were acting how Keaton had said they would—warm and welcoming to a Taylor daughter.

But Jake needed to get his mom to stop talking. Now.

"Let me get Skye back to the couch," he said to Gloria. "Then I'll come help put away the groceries."

"Oh, I can—" Jake cut her off with a look that he hoped like hell said, *Go into the kitchen, please.* "Ah. Yes. Groceries. Then we'll have lunch!" She headed into the other room.

Jake walked Skye over to the couch.

"They seem nice?" she said.

And he couldn't help it. He loved this woman. He wanted…he wanted so much with this Skye. But what would happen when she got those two years back? "I think they're really trying," he said with a quick kiss. "Lunch?"

She leaned back with a dreamy smile on her face. "Lunch sounds good," she called after him as he hurried to the kitchen before his mother could do something else that put everything at risk.

"How is she?" Gloria asked in a quiet voice as

she opened the cabinet doors to find a place to put a box of spaghetti. "She looks a lot better."

"She is better—but the doctor said that we can't overload her with information right now. She's lost about two years and I'm not supposed to tell her what she's forgotten. She's supposed to remember it on her own."

His mother paused, another box of pasta in her hand. "What did happen in those two years, Jake? Heavens, those four years?"

Great. Wonderful. Just when he thought things couldn't get any worse. Time to go with the supershort version. "We got married. I started a company. We lived in Houston, but I traveled for work. Skye had a freelance graphic design business."

His mother nodded her head thoughtfully. "Is that where you've been for the last four months? On a job?"

Jake shut his eyes and breathed deeply, trying to find the calm. He would not get into a fight with his mother. A fight would upset Skye and, after all, his parents were trying to help. He could cook for Skye now. That was a good thing.

"I was in Bahrain," he told her. "In the Middle East, working on IT for an oil-production facility."

Then, because his mother was obviously not buying this as a good-enough reason for the radio silence while Skye had been hospitalized, he added, "I was contractually bound to stay there and finish the job. Skye knew that. She didn't want to go to Bahrain. We had agreed, but she's forgotten all about Bahrain and I *really* don't think reminding her of it is the best thing for her mental well-being right now so please, for the love of God, go easy on her. As far as she remembers, the fight at Claire's is still kind of fresh in her mind."

His mother just regarded him with that all-knowing look that had always spelled trouble back when he was a kid sneaking out past his bedtime to meet Skye. But she didn't nag, thank heavens. Instead, she said, "All right, dear. I'll keep it light. Can I talk about Grace?"

"Yes, but I haven't taken Skye to see her yet. I was going to let her get a day of rest under her belt first. It's fine if you talk about Grace, but don't ask about the pregnancy. Skye doesn't remember any of it and I don't want to stress her out."

Just then, David Holt came back in with another armful of groceries and the covered dish Gloria had been using for church socials since probably before Jake had been born. David glanced at the two of them and said, "Everything okay in here?"

"Fine," Jake said. And that? That was a lie. Not a gloss, not a half-truth. A flat-out lie.

Nothing was fine now. He was living with a woman who didn't remember falling out of love with him. He was standing in a kitchen in Royal, Texas, talking to his parents. Less than two miles away, his brother was probably singing Jake's daughter to sleep.

Jake had no idea what was going to happen next month, next week, tomorrow—hell, at the rate he was going, the next ten minutes were going to be chock-full of surprises. At this point, even Bigfoot ringing his doorbell wouldn't be *that* astounding.

"Sweetie," Gloria said, sounding…nice about it? "I know this has probably been a lot."

"Yeah," he agreed, wondering if he was actually on the verge of apologizing to his parents. His parents, for God's sake. "I'm sorry. I'm just worried sick about Skye and trying to figure out how to take care of her and Grace and not lose my business in the process."

"Are you all talking about me or what?" Skye called out from the living room.

"Sorry," Jake called back. He saw that his dad had carried in a variety pack of tea. "Thirsty? We have tea now."

"Please," Skye called back. "You know how I like it."

Jake went to find the kettle, but somehow, his mother beat him to it. "Go on," she said, shooing him out of the kitchen. "You two have a lot to catch up on. I'll get lunch ready and we'll all eat together."

*Great.* He wasn't looking forward to it, but on the other hand, the longer his parents stayed here, the less opportunity there'd be to find Skye so... *tempting.* "That sounds good."

Jake went to sit next to Skye. "How is it in there?" she asked in a worried voice. "Are they mad at us?"

"No, babe," he said, taking her hand in his. "I think..." He sighed. "I think they've changed. Grace helped."

"So they're not upset? Really? Oh, Jake—that's great!" She leaned her head against his shoulder. "I always hoped we'd be able to come back, you know."

He was going to get an ulcer at this point. He

did, in fact, know that. Skye hadn't said much about it their first two years together, but after that?

Yeah, she'd started voicing that hope. She wanted to be able to come home, see if maybe their families would be able to accept that she and Jake were married. And Jake had had no interest in even testing the waters. He wouldn't say it was *the* issue that drove a wedge between them, but it was still a spike that got hammered into that wedge.

"I know," he told her, mostly because he couldn't think of a better evasion. He wanted to go through the list of reasons why he didn't want to stay here—but he didn't want to upset her, especially not after dressing down his mother for the exact same reason. "We'll...we'll visit. When you're better and Grace is stronger, we'll—"

"But Jake," she said and he knew he was doing a lousy job of tap-dancing around the truth of the matter. "I thought we might, you know, be able to move back here. To come home. This would be a great place to raise Grace..." Her brow wrinkled. "When can I see her?"

"Let's get through the night," he told her. "This

is your first day home, after all—I don't want you to overdo it. If you feel up to it tomorrow, I'll call Lark and we'll go over."

These were all perfectly reasonable responses. So why did he feel so bad about saying them?

Hell, he didn't know. He didn't know anything anymore.

He knew even less when Gloria came out carrying a plate loaded with her famous chicken enchilada casserole and a napkin for Skye. Jake got his own plate and they all sat around and ate and chatted as if the past two years hadn't happened—not to mention the last decade.

His mother was warm and effusive—she managed to keep the conversation light, as promised—and his father let his mother do the talking. There was something comforting about it. No one accused him of betraying the Holt family name to consort with a no-good Taylor. No one tried to convince him to drop Skye for "a nice girl." It was almost…normal. It was how it should have been all those years ago.

Which was great, but also another obstacle he was going to have to deal with sooner or later. Because this was exactly the sort of family interaction Skye had wanted more and more, and if she thought this was the new normal, she was going to demand it long after she recovered.

And Jake...

He wanted his wife back. The wife she was being right now—not the quiet, resentful woman she'd morphed into over the past couple of years.

Would he even consider moving back to this town? To just acting as if the past had blown away in a tornado—like they were doing right now?

"I'll get these things," Gloria said, gathering up the plates after they'd finished the meal.

"I'll help," Jake offered.

For a moment, he thought his mother was going to refuse his help, but then she and his father exchanged a look. David gave her a little nod and she said, "Why, that'd be nice. Will you two be okay?"

"Sure," harrumphed David as he dug out his phone. "I can show Skye pictures of Grace, if that's okay."

"That should be fine..." Jake said nervously as he followed Gloria into the kitchen.

"You have pictures?" Skye gasped.

Suddenly, this seemed like a bad idea. He knew

he couldn't filter Skye's world for forever, but... well, his father had always been a man of few words. Surely he wouldn't set Skye off, would he?

Gloria already had the dishes in the dishwasher by the time he got in there with his own. Jake wasn't sure what he was supposed to say—were they still keeping it light? "Thanks again for getting groceries. How much were they?"

Gloria waved him off. "Don't worry about it."

"Mom, I'm going to pay you back. That was at least a hundred bucks' worth of groceries. I didn't expect for you to foot the bill." Already, his irritation was growing. He should have stayed in the living room.

She leaned against the counter, a stern look on her face and her arms crossed over her ample chest. He knew he wasn't going to win this argument. "It's a small price to pay to make up for how we treated you two," she said in a matter-of-fact kind of way.

*"What?"*

"We shouldn't have forced you to choose. I guess that, deep down, I knew that if you'd stayed on the ranch with us, you'd have come to hate us for driving Skye away. We wasted a lot of time trying to keep you two apart and it never did us a lick of good."

Jake stood there, gaping at her. "Really?"

From the living room came the sound of a happy Skye going, "Awwww! Look at her tiny hands!"

Jake tried to regain his footing. "Why are you apologizing now?"

"Why do you think? You're here. Keaton said you weren't planning on disappearing again, but this has troubled my conscience for the last four years—your father's, too, although he's still too stubborn to admit it. We've missed you terribly."

"Mom, I don't know what to say." He scrubbed a hand through his hair. "I—I didn't think you missed us at all." Actually, after that last fight? He'd been operating under the assumption that not only did his parents not miss him, but they were actively glad Jake was gone.

"And her feet!" came the gushing squeal from the living room.

"Oh, now." His mother brushed aside his comment with a wave of her hand. "Of course we did. Your father took your leaving real hard. He did a lot of soul searching about the land dispute and realized it wasn't worth losing his son over."

*"Really?"* Because that was not the impression Jake had gotten when his father had said, *Either you're with us or against us.*

His mother looked at him as if she were really seeing him as an adult for the first time. "Of course, that was before the tornado knocked down town hall."

"What? What does that have to do with anything?"

She gave him a small smile, but there was no joy in it. "As they cleared away the rubble, they found the original land deed that shows the Taylors moved the fences."

What had he thought earlier today, about not even knowing what the next ten minutes had in store for him? Because he'd pretty much nailed it. "So—what, Tyrone Taylor just gave the land back?"

"Oh, no. I believe he's claiming the deed was forged—that sort of thing. There's probably going to be a lawsuit. Keaton is handling that. But you being gone and then your father being proved right—well, it's taken the fight out of him. Especially now."

In the background, Skye cried out, "She's so *small*! Oh…"

"Why now?"

"Why, Grace, of course. And I expect that Lark and Keaton will start a family before too much longer. To see Lark with Grace…" Gloria sighed in contentment. "The land will go to our family no matter what."

"So…now what?"

"That's what I was going to ask you," she said. "Will you two stay?"

What would it take for a bolt of lightning to strike out of the blue and fry him where he stood? Because being electrocuted had to be more fun than this conversation. "Mom, we have a life in Houston."

"I know, I know. But I'd sure love to have my grandbaby close by while we're still here. Keaton told you we're thinking of retiring to Alabama?"

"Yeah, he mentioned something about that." It hadn't made any sense at the time, but now— knowing that the feud was all but over and that his father wasn't going to fight Tyrone Taylor any- more? It made a lot more sense now.

"If you stayed, you two could move into the ranch house. It'd be a great place to raise a family."

*If.* That was one hell of an *if.* Jake hadn't wanted to stay because he wanted nothing to go with his family or the feud.

But if the feud was close to being resolved and half of his relatives were going to be living in Alabama, of all places...

It was still a huge *if.* "I just need to focus on Skye and Grace right now. But," he added when his mother busted out her disappointed face, "I'll think about it."

She beamed at him. "Thank you, dear."

"Jake?" Skye called out. "You've got to come see these!"

Jake was grateful for the out. He and Gloria headed back to the living room, where David was sitting next to Skye and holding his phone so she could see it. "Babe, look," Skye said. Her eyes were welling up with tears. "That's our girl."

The photo was of an impossibly small baby—so swaddled that Jake could barely see her face—lying in Gloria's arms. David was crouched down next to her, the silliest grin Jake had ever seen on the man's face. "Wow," he said. Had he ever seen his parents look so happy? Not when it involved a Taylor, that was for sure.

"Jake said if I was feeling up to it, we'd go see her tomorrow. Lark's got her." Skye sounded enthusiastic as she said it, but there was no missing the yawn she tried to hide behind her hand.

"Take pictures," Gloria ordered. "We'll send you these."

"Oh, good. I want to do baby announcements and everything. I've missed so much..." She looked up at Jake. "I feel like I've missed years."

He didn't want her to get those years back, which was selfish and shortsighted, but it was what it was. He wanted her to stay like this. He didn't want her to remember that he hadn't been enough to keep her happy, that she'd wanted something more.

"Well," Gloria announced, "you need your rest. But you call us if you need anything, you hear?"

"Thanks, Mom." He walked them out to their car. "It's...it's been good to see you again."

And the funny thing was, he wasn't sure if that was a lie or not. He just didn't know anymore.

He wasn't that surprised when his mom hugged him, but when his dad hugged him? Yeah, that wasn't what he'd expected. "Son," David said, "I'm—well, I'm glad you're home."

Which was probably as close to an actual apology as Jake would ever get out of the old man. "Me, too, Dad."

He was stunned to see the old man's eyes watering when David abruptly let him go a second later. "We'll be seeing you," he said gruffly and all but ran to the car.

Gloria shot Jake an I-told-you-so smile and waved before she got in the passenger side.

Once they were gone, Jake stood there and tried to process everything. The storm, the baby, the feud, his family, Skye's family—and Skye. Always, he came back to Skye.

She'd remember, wouldn't she? And when she did…he might very well lose her again.

He didn't want to lose her again. He'd already lost her once—nearly twice, in that accident. Could he do what it would take to keep her? Even if it meant dealing with everything, all at once again?

Was this how Skye felt? That suddenly there was so much new information to process and none of it made a lick of sense?

He couldn't stand out here all day—that much was for sure. What if Skye got it into her head to come look for him? She wasn't steady enough yet.

When he got back into the house, he saw that Skye had her eyes closed. She opened them when he shut the door. "I don't remember your parents being that nice, but they wore me out. I think I need a nap."

"Good plan." If she slept, he could finish up his email.

"Will you snuggle with me?" She held up her arms—not in the way that said she wanted him to help her stand, but in the way that made it clear that she wanted him to pick her up like he had last night. "Please?"

The answer should be *no*. A firm *no*. He had things to do and he was having enough trouble keeping his hands off of her to begin with.

"Please, Jake. You're right—I'm too tired to do anything right now. Including walk."

How could he say no to her? He couldn't. He *couldn't*. And he was tired, too. His head couldn't process anything on the little sleep he'd gotten last night.

So he swept her into his arms and carried her

upstairs. She rested her head against his shoulder and yawned. "We'll try to see Grace tomorrow, right?"

"Right," he agreed as he carried Skye into the bedroom and set her down on the bed. Then he kicked off his shoes and slid in next to her, pulling the covers up over both of them.

He wrapped his body around hers, and buried his nose in her hair. He shouldn't be in bed with her, shouldn't be holding her tight. He absolutely should *not* be thinking about ways he could make this work.

He didn't know how to make it work, though. What about his business? What about the jobs he'd bid on?

And their families. If he fought for her again, he'd have to deal with his family and hers. Maybe his family had changed. Maybe, instead of the death sentence that coming back to Royal had always felt like, it'd be…tolerable.

Could he do tolerable? Could he do it for her? For them?

Her body relaxed into sleep in his arms and he found himself thinking of their wedding. Of finally having escaped from the oppressive feud, of no longer giving a damn what their families thought. Just Jake and Skye, together—forever.

This was forever, wasn't it?

He could not lose her again. He didn't know who he was without Skye. The ten months in Bahrain had been so far beyond hell on earth—he'd been little more than a zombie. He'd left half of himself behind when he'd left her. Plus, she was now the mother of his child.

Maybe he was too tired to be making decisions. Maybe he should get up, go back downstairs and get some work done. Maybe he should still try to keep his distance from her...

Or maybe he should fight for her. For them. He should show her that, no matter what happened in the past, whether she remembered it or not, he would always be here for her.

And then, maybe when she remembered how they fell apart, it'd be tempered by the new memories of how they'd put themselves back together.

He could love her again. He could give her what she wanted. He could *be* what she wanted. Because if he didn't at least try, she would be gone. Again.

He pulled her in close and kissed her on the forehead.

He *wouldn't* let that happen.

He just wouldn't.

# Seven

Skye was floating through yet another dream—this time, Jake was lying next to her in bed, his arms around her, his warmth surrounding her.

She was so tired of this dream. It was a nice dream, but she wanted it to be real. She wanted the real Jake, not just the ghost of him that drifted through her sleep. "I want you to be real," she sighed in frustration.

"I am," he replied, kissing her on the neck. "I'm right here, my blue-eyed Skye."

As his lips moved over hers, his hands skimmed over her back and down to her bottom, where he squeezed. Languid heat began to build in her body—which wasn't something she remembered happening with Dream Jake. Dream Jake had always slipped between her fingers, leaving her frustrated and alone.

When he nipped at her earlobe, she felt more than just a foggy touch. She felt his teeth.

She was awake. This was really happening. She hoped. Oh, how she hoped. "Jake?"

He cupped her face in his hands and kissed her again—on the forehead this time. "I want you so much, but I want you to want me, too."

She blinked the last bits of sleep from her eyes. What was he talking about? She'd done nothing but want him since he'd walked into the hospital two days ago. "Of course I want you. The accident didn't change that. Nothing could."

"You're sure?" He looked so serious about it. "Because I'm not going to let you go."

How could he even say something like that—about letting her go? She had the feeling that he was talking about something else—but she couldn't grasp what it was.

Or maybe he was just talking about the coma she'd been in. Yes, that made more sense. "You were all I thought about."

Guilt—which was not a sensual emotion—

washed over his face. "Skye..." But instead of explaining why he looked guilty, he pulled her into a fierce hug. "I will always come back for you," he whispered into her hair. "Always. You are mine."

Something in the embrace turned from emotional to erotic. His body started to rock against her and she clung to him, praying that no one would stop by or call or do anything to interrupt them. This time was theirs and she didn't want to miss another moment with him.

"My blue-eyed Skye," he murmured against her lips before he kissed her.

"Oh, Jake," she groaned. "I love you."

He growled as she nipped at his lower lip. He pulled away and grabbed the hem of her shirt. It came off easily without even touching most of her hair. Skye made a grab for Jake's buttons, but he captured her hands in his. "You first," he said. "I want to see you so bad."

He slid the lounge pants over her hips, leaving her in nothing but the cotton panties. He looked her over, naked hunger in his eyes. "You are *so* beautiful," he said again and she knew he telling the truth. "The most beautiful woman I've ever seen."

He leaned into her, his hands skimming over her arms, her shoulders and down her back. His touch was light and warm, but she shivered, anyway. "Jake…"

He worked the panties off her hips. "I want to kiss you over every square inch of your body until you can't even breathe," he murmured against her neck.

"Oh, my," she said, angling her head back so he could have better access. Her legs were aching from propping herself up against him, but she didn't want to pull away. Not yet. Not when she finally had him back in her arms. "I think that can be arranged."

This time, when she went for his shirt buttons, he didn't try to stop her. Her fingers seemed to have forgotten the basic mechanics of undressing a man, because they fumbled with the first button. "I can do this," she told him in frustration as she failed to get yet another button on the first try. She didn't want to get hung up on this step—what if there was another interruption? She couldn't bear it. She just *couldn't*.

He tilted her head up. "Don't mind me," he said with a serious look in his eye. "I'm just watching you be naked. Trust me, the view from here?" He whistled.

She grinned at him as some of her nervousness faded. He was always doing that, finding a way to put her at ease. No matter what, he was still her Jake. Finally, she got the danged buttons undone and slid the shirt off his arms.

"Oh," she breathed as the hard planes of his chest were laid bare for her to see. She stroked her fingers over the fine hairs that covered his chest and arms, then leaned up and pressed a kiss to his chest.

Jake sucked in a hot breath. "Oh, I missed you, too."

But when she went for his belt buckle, he grabbed her hands again. "Don't," he gritted out, "don't want it over too soon."

Skye giggled again. "I remember..." she said as Jake crawled between her legs. "I remember this."

"Yeah?" he asked as he dropped his mouth to her breast. "Tell me what you remember, babe."

"I remember..." There were images floating around her head, all muddled up with the heated desire he was unleashing upon her body. Her brain might not be operating at full capacity, but her body seemed to have a better recall. Muscle memory, she wanted to call it. Because her muscles remembered. "I remember the first time you touched my breasts. And I was—oh, Jake!" she gasped as he scraped his teeth over her nipple.

"Go on," he murmured against her skin as he shifted to the other breast. "Tell me what you remember."

"I was nervous because—because I was so small and you were unhooking my bra and…and…" They'd been teenagers, nervous and fumbling in the front seat of his truck—wanting *so* much and afraid of it, too. Afraid that the further she went with Jake, the less they'd be friends. Afraid that he'd get her padded bra off of her and see how little she really had and it wouldn't be enough for him. But the need to be with him then—just like now—had been too strong to ignore. He'd gotten her bra unhooked and looked at her small breasts and said—

"And I said you were perfect," he finished for her. "Perfect for me." Then he rolled her nipple between his tongue and teeth. "Because you are, Skye. You are the only woman for me."

"Jake," she moaned. She did remember this—how he'd always lavished attention on her breasts, made her feel special instead of lacking.

But things were different now, too. Her nipples were tight and hot under his kisses, but it didn't feel exactly the way she remembered it. Was that because she was remembering wrong, or because her body had changed?

"I *love* your body," he said, his mouth trailing down her belly.

He was almost to the C-section scar—a thin, angry red line that stood out like a flashing light on her pale skin. "Even—that?"

He found the scar and kissed the length of it. "Even this. This gave us our daughter. Your body is amazing. This isn't a scar, babe. It's a tattoo of strength and I don't ever want you to be ashamed of it."

Her throat closed up at his sweet words. "Oh, Jake…"

But that was as far as she got before he moved lower. Jake ran his hands up and down her legs as he sat back and adjusted her hips. He leaned down and pressed a kiss to her inner thigh, then he put his mouth against her sex and began to stroke her with his tongue. "Oh, Jake!"

He sat back on his heels, but didn't stop touching her. Instead of his mouth, his fingers began to rub over her. The heat was anything but languid now. Skye began to writhe.

Skye was filled with warmth and lightness. This was the man she loved—the man who could strip her down and lay her out and make her want him. She couldn't remember being as happy as she was right now.

Then he slipped a finger inside of her.

Skye's hips twisted as she responded to his touch. It was more than she was used to—but not enough. She needed even more. "Jake," she groaned, desperate for something to hold on to.

Then his mouth was on her again and there was nothing slow or funny about what he was doing to her body. She ran her fingers through his hair and held on as he worked her up to the point where she couldn't hold back. The orgasm hit her with so much force that she came all the way off the bed as she cried out, "Jake!"

"Oh, babe," he moaned from between her legs. "I've missed you so much. *So* much."

She fell back onto the bed, panting. "How could I forget?" Then she managed to lift her left foot and nudge at the huge erection that was straining behind his jeans. "Might need a refresher on *that*," she tried to say in a joking tone.

"Woman," he growled again as he shoved himself away from her. He yanked his jeans off, along with his boxers.

"Don't stop," she moaned. "Babe, don't stop."

But he looked at her, his eyes wide.

And he stopped.

What the hell was he doing?

Jake stared at her. His blood was pounding in his ears—and a few other places—and he could still taste her sweetness on his tongue. He'd—he'd decided to fight for her. That realization emerged from the haze that was his brain.

But…should he really be having sex with her? At least, right now? Shouldn't he give it another week—another day—so she could recover? Shouldn't he be putting her needs above his own?

"Jake?" She was staring at him with those huge

blue eyes of hers. *Perfect*. She was just perfect. Always had been. And he'd always had so much trouble saying no to her.

She lifted herself up and hesitantly wrapped her fingers around him. He shuddered at her touch, but he was powerless to put the brakes on, powerless to do anything but love her. Slowly—so slowly it was driving all reason out of his mind—she stroked him. And this time, there was no doorbell to save him from her. From himself. "It's okay. I've waited too long for this."

If only she knew how long she'd been waiting.

"But what if—?" What if he got her pregnant *again*?

"Then I'll remember. Oh, babe, I want you so much." She stroked up, down, up again and it obliterated any reasonable thought. He hadn't had sex in over ten months. Ten months without this woman under him—beside him—on top of him. It felt like a lifetime. He couldn't stand it anymore. Not when she was here, loving on him like this.

He gently pushed her back onto the bed and lowered his mouth to her breasts again. She'd always been a little insecure about how small she was, so he made sure that she knew how much he loved her just as she was.

Soon enough, she was shifting underneath him, lifting her hips up so that she could be closer to him. "Jake," she begged. "Jake, *please.*"

He fell into her. He couldn't stay away from her—he'd never been able to. His father had punished him each time Jake and Skye had been caught together. Jake had gone to college a year before she had. He'd gone to Bahrain without her. But he'd come back for her. He would *always* come back for her.

He didn't want to crush her slim body, so he propped himself up on his hands and fit himself against her.

"Jake," she hissed as he teased her with his tip. *"Jake."*

He couldn't hold himself back, not with her tantalizing warmth surrounding him. He thrust into her, gently at first, but then her fingernails found his back, spurring him on. *"Mine,"* he said as he surrendered to her. "My blue-eyed Skye."

"Oh, yes," she gasped out as her body tightened around his. He buried himself in her over and over again. Nothing between them. Not now, not ever.

He sat back on his heels and pulled her hips down into his, thrusting hard. "Skye," he ground out.

Then she cried out his name and it pushed him over the edge. With the last bit of self-control he had, he pulled out as he came. Condoms. He was going to have to get some condoms immediately.

He collapsed onto the bed next to her and drew her into his arms. They were both breathing hard. "I love you, Skye," he said low and close to her ear. "Nothing—not even comas—can change that. I've loved you since I was seven and I will love you to the day I draw in my last breath."

"I don't ever want us to be apart, Jake." Her breath hitched her chest up. "Even when I was asleep, I missed you so much. Don't ever leave me again."

He froze. Was she remembering something—or was she still operating under the assumption that he'd just been in New York for a job for a while?

He *hated* this. There were many things that had gone wrong between them, but lying hadn't been one of them. They were always honest with each other. Even if he was only glossing over the truth, it still sat wrong in his craw.

He knew he needed to tell her about the past two years—he couldn't keep secrets, not from her. He *knew* that it would be better if she heard it from him before she remembered it on her own.

But he couldn't. Not just yet. After all, on her first full day home from the hospital, she'd not only had to deal with surprise visits from neighbors, but from his family as well—well-meaning as they were. Then he'd ravished her, essentially.

She had to be exhausted and the last thing she needed was another emotional shock. They'd have time to discuss everything that had happened right before her accident later. After they'd settled into the house and she'd gotten some of her strength back and they'd had a chance to spend a little time with Grace.

He had time to show her what she meant to him before the past caught up with them. A week, maybe. Skye would be much better by then.

He hoped. God, he hoped.

# Eight

"Can we go now?" Skye asked for the fourteenth time that morning.

"Noon," Jake repeated. And then, because he was having trouble keeping his hands off of her, he leaned over as she held her leg lifts and kissed her. "Just a little bit longer."

Skye was not mollified by this announcement. She'd woken up in a good mood, but once Jake had gotten her back on the floor do to the exercises, that mood had turned into impatience. "I just want to see her," Skye said as she struggled her way through the exercises. "I just want to hold her."

"I know," he repeated, trying to keep her calm.

"Lark said to come over at noon. We still have three hours. Let's stretch."

He couldn't believe it, but as he stood over her and lifted her leg toward the ceiling, he found himself flirting with her. Yesterday, he'd been desperate to not flirt with her. But today? It was the best weapon he had in keeping her distracted. "Maybe we should try this in bed," he joked.

That got him a funny look. "And how do you suggest we pull *that* off?"

"I have my ways." She laughed, which he took as a good sign. "Here, roll over." He began to give her a massage.

"Mmm, good," she murmured as he worked at a knot in her shoulder. "I hadn't realized how tight I was."

Jake laughed. This was the Skye he'd run off with—the one who could make a suggestive joke and tell him what she wanted.

When she rolled back over again, he couldn't help himself. He lowered himself to her and kissed her. "As a reward," he murmured against her neck.

"You make me wish I was doing PT three times a day," she said as she grinned up at him.

She started to deepen the kiss—and Jake was

tempted to let it go on—but they had to leave the house today. So he sat back and pulled her into a sitting position. "Shower?"

Her eyebrows jumped. "Together?"

"If that's what you want." He kept asking her variations on that—did she want to watch this? Do that? Eat that?

But what he was really asking was if she wanted him. He wasn't going to sit around and watch them fall apart again. When she remembered—it was just a matter of time—then he wanted her to have some new, better memories to counterbalance the bad ones. Memories in which he'd taken care of her—in which he'd still loved her, still fought for her.

She would remember that he'd left. He wanted her to remember that he'd come back for her and for Grace.

He helped her into the bathroom. She was getting stronger, he could tell—despite the hard workout, she was able to get undressed on her own. Jake stripped out of his own clothes and helped her to sit on the bench after he got the water to the right temperature. The shower was roomy and the showerhead could be removed from the wall so he was able to rinse her hair. "I'll try to put it back like it was," he offered.

She leaned back, her head resting on his stomach. "Try?"

"*Try.*" Then he had her lean forward so that he could wash her back again.

"You know," she said in a casual way, "I kind of thought you were avoiding me when you gave me that bath."

Jake froze, but then thought that might trigger something in her mind, so he went on lathering up her body. "Why would you think that?"

She managed to pivot and look up at him. "I thought…it just seemed like you didn't want me. I was afraid maybe I'd done something I couldn't remember that, you know, wasn't so good."

"I did want you. I *do*," he hurried to say. "Honestly, I was afraid of hurting you." Which, again, was not the whole truth. But there was some truth to it. "All I want is for you to get better, faster. I don't want to do anything that might mess that up."

She beamed at him. "Okay, good." She took the soap. "Now it's my turn."

"What do you—*oh*." Skye ran the soap over his

body and, damn it all, he went hard in an instant at her touch. "Skye—you don't have to do this."

"Who said anything about having to?" she demanded as she stroked him. "I want to. You're taking care of me. Let me take care of you."

"I don't—want you—to overdo—it," he ground out as she worked on him. So she'd lost two years. She remembered what he liked—the strong, sure strokes. Then she rinsed him off and ran her tongue over his tip. "Like this?" she murmured, her voice vibrating up through him.

"Just like that," he managed to say. He leaned forward and braced his hands on the wall of the shower as she licked his tip and stroked his length and did everything she could to drive him wild with lust.

"Skye," he warned her as he tried to pull back. "Wait—let me—"

"No," she said as she held fast to him. "You, Jake Holt, are *mine*."

She claimed him then—took everything he had to give as the orgasm almost brought him to his knees.

Hell, it actually did—he sank down in front of her and clutched her to his chest as he waited for his pulse to return to normal. "My perfect Skye," he got out.

"Was it okay?"

He looked at her. "Okay? No." Her face started to crumble, so he quickly said, "Great? *Yes.*"

He was hers. She'd said so herself.

He gave her a wicked grin. "Your turn."

Before she knew what was happening, Jake had parted her legs, grabbed her by the thighs and pulled her so that she was barely sitting on the bench. "Perfect," he murmured again as his mouth closed in on her.

The warm water cascaded down over them as he worked his tongue over her and his fingers into her. Maybe yesterday he had been worried about hurting her—holding back just a little, just in case.

He did no such thing today. Her body, already relaxed from the shower, gave itself over to his touches as they came harder, faster—

"Jake!"

"Come for me, babe," he said against her sex. "Come for me."

So she did. Her body lit up as the desire overwhelmed her. *Alive*. She was alive and getting stronger here with Jake. It was all she'd ever wanted.

After one of the longer—and better—showers in recent memory, Skye finally got into a clean set of clothes and Jake mostly got her hair brushed back over into a side ponytail. Skye didn't even attempt eyeliner or mascara—her arms were already tired and she wanted to save her strength for holding Grace—but she managed to put on a little makeup without Jake's help. Gloria had asked for pictures, after all. Skye wanted to look as normal as possible.

"Ready?" Jake asked, a big smile on his face.

She nodded. It felt good to know that she'd put that smile there, that he'd returned the favor. She didn't remember them having a bench in the bathroom in their apartment, but if they moved back here to Royal permanently, they'd have to make sure they had a bench in their new home.

She wanted to tell Jake that—but something held her back. Jake had made his position quite clear—he was never coming back to Royal. She remembered *that*. But hadn't that been because of his family? Well, her family, too.

They'd had a lovely lunch with his parents—people so warm and friendly that she almost couldn't believe they were the same two who had forced Jake to choose between the Holt ranch and Skye. And now, after a careful trip down the stairs and out to the car, they were going to go see Keaton and Lark and…

Grace.

Skye's heart tried to skip a beat at just the thought of the tiny baby in all the pictures David had showed her.

"Nervous?" Jake asked her as he backed out of the driveway. "Or just excited?"

"Both," she admitted. "I hope I don't drop her!"

"I don't think that'll happen," he assured her. "We'll get you set up on Lark's couch and you can just hold the baby."

"I hope I can feed her," Skye said. "I want to help take care of her."

Jake shot her a silly look. "You may want to avoid diaper duty for a while longer. I'm just saying, I may be emotionally scarred for life from *that*."

Skye laughed at him. "Jake," she said, feeling

light and free. "I don't know if I've ever been this happy."

All the silliness bled out of his face. "We were happy," he told her. "When it was just the two of us."

"Oh, I know—I don't mean that we weren't. I love living with you. It's just, well, you know—our families are getting along and we have a baby now. I secretly hoped that this would happen."

At least, she'd thought it was secret. But Jake said heavily, "Yeah, I know."

"You do?" She didn't remember telling him that. In fact, she'd thought she'd done a very good job hiding that from him because she knew that he'd never wanted to come back here.

"I mean," he quickly corrected, "I suspected as much." All serious now, he looked over at her. "Do you still want to come back here?"

At least, that's what he said. But deep inside one of the holes in Skye's memory, she heard a different question.

*Why do you still want to go back there?*

She tried to grab hold of that other question, that other memory—but she couldn't. "I don't know," she admitted. "You're right—we've been so happy on our own. But there's things I missed—having a friendly neighbor fix my hair or lunch with your folks, or my sister babysitting so we can… shower together." She gave him what she hoped was a coy smile, but the stony look on his face rebuffed her advance. "It's not something I want to fight about, Jake."

His jaw worked, as if he was trying to say something and also not trying to say something at the same time, which left her greatly confused. What was in that damn hole in her memory? What couldn't she grasp? "Jake?"

"You know," he said through clenched teeth, which undermined the casual tone of his voice, "you've only been home for a few days. We're going to be here for a month, maybe—your doctor wants you to stay close. So let's not worry about this right now. Let's just focus on you getting better and seeing Grace, okay?"

She looked down at her hands. All the light, happy feelings from the shower earlier were gone now. "Did I do something wrong?"

"Of course not," he said. "I don't know about you, but this has been a pretty awesome day. Especially the shower part."

"I don't mean that. I mean…am I forgetting something I did? Did we have a fight?" He didn't answer, but she could tell he was gripping the steering wheel with enough force to break it off the column. "Is that…?" She swallowed, her throat suddenly closing up on her. "Is that why you weren't with me when I hit that storm?"

Jake didn't reply, but then, he was pulling into another driveway. He put the car in park and leaned over. "You were pregnant," he told her as he cupped her face in his hand. "You didn't want to travel to the job with me. I think you'd decided to come see Lark while I was gone."

Suddenly she had tears in her eyes. "Did we fight?"

His mouth opened, but instead of answering her question, he leaned over and kissed her. She let him because she couldn't remember what she couldn't remember, but Jake's love surpassed it all. "Whatever happened in the past isn't as important as what happens in the future, Skye."

"But—"

Just then, the door to the house opened up and there stood her sister with a small bundle in her arms. "Skye?"

"Oh!" What were they doing, sitting here and having…well, a conversation, although a highly strange one, when their daughter was just over there? "We should go."

"Yup," he agreed, getting out and coming over to her side of the car.

She wanted to walk on her own two feet. She didn't want to be too weak even to walk to her own daughter. But her left leg tried to buckle on the fourth step and Jake had to put his arm around her waist and half carry her to the door.

But the frustration at not being able to use her body in a normal, typical way disappeared in an instant as Skye looked down at the baby in Lark's arms. "Oh, Grace," she said, choking up. "My little bit of Grace."

The baby—with bright blue eyes and almost no hair—was looking around, as if everything were new and surprising. "Come inside," Lark said. "I don't want her to get too cold, but we were waiting for you—weren't we, Grace?"

Skye and Jake followed Lark as she led the way into a large room filled with every kind of baby toy imaginable. "I don't—*we* don't have any of this stuff," Skye said. She'd been so focused on just getting her strength back up to the point where she could carry Grace that she hadn't even considered all the things a baby required.

"Don't worry about that," Lark said with a suspicious grin. "Come over and sit down. She's due for a bottle in about half an hour. I'll show you how to prop your legs up so you can talk to her."

Lark and Jake traded places. "You look great," Lark said as she helped Skye down onto one side of a couch that had tall sides. "I mean, you look really great."

"Thanks. Um…what was her name?"

"Megan," Jake said without looking up. "Megan Maguire. Engaged to Whit Daltry. How's Daddy's little girl today, huh?" he cooed to Grace.

"Megan bought me some clothes and makeup and brushed my hair so it hid the short spots. I feel almost normal, you know?"

"It's wonderful," Lark said. "Here." She extended the footrest and adjusted the height so that Skye was tilted back a bit. "Now, bend your knees up—yes, like that. Let me just lay down this blanket—perfect." She turned to Jake. "Ready?"

"Yup."

Skye's chest clenched at the huge grin on Jake's

face as he looked down at their daughter. He loved Grace. Oh, that made her so happy she was on the verge of crying again.

Jake slid down on the couch next to her. "Say hi to Mommy, sweetie," he said as he laid Grace in Skye's arms.

She couldn't help it. The happiest tears of her life cascaded down her cheeks. "Hi, Grace," she said, her voice shaking with emotion.

"She's beautiful," Jake said. "Just like her mother."

"I wanted her for so long," Skye said. "*So* long. You have no idea."

"I do, babe. I do." Jake slid his arm around her shoulder and held her close. Grace opened her eyes wide as she looked up at both of them and made a cooing noise.

"She likes you more than she likes me," Jake told her. "The first time I held her, she gave me a 'present.'"

"I'm still laughing about that one," Lark said. She sat down in an easy chair that was close enough to the couch that she could sweep in and snag Grace if Skye lost her grip.

Not that Skye had any plans to do that. She held

Grace tightly, feeling the little muscles moving underneath the blanket. "How is she?" she asked Lark. "I mean, what's she like?"

"She sleeps a lot," Lark replied. She wore a satisfied grin on her face. Skye wasn't sure she'd ever seen her sister look so happy. "That's typical of preemies. And her lungs are still developing. It's risky for her to be around a bunch of new people. We don't want her to get sick."

Grace made a little grunting noise in the back of her throat and both Skye and Jake startled. "What's wrong?" they said at the same time. But even as she asked it, Skye thought the noises seemed familiar. Had she heard them before?

Lark laughed. "Nothing—she's fine, I promise. That's just a noise a lot of preemies make. She's almost caught up to her gestational age—how developed she would have been if she'd been full term. She likes to make that noise when I put her on the ground."

"What?" Jake said. Skye could tell that he didn't exactly like that idea.

"Tummy time," Lark said, motioning toward the floor. "She needs to spend a few minutes on her tummy every few hours. It'll help her build her neck strength and keep the back of her head from getting flat."

"Oh." Skye saw a square mat decorated with black and white swirls and red ladybugs. "Okay. That's good to know. I guess we'll get something like that—right, Jake?"

"Absolutely," he said.

Grace made a different sounding grunt. "Oh, here—she wants to look around," Lark said. "Are your legs stable?"

"I…guess?"

Lark leaned over and shifted Grace from Skye's arms so that the baby was almost sitting upright between Skye's thighs. Lark then undid the swaddled blankets a little so that Grace's impossibly tiny hands were free. "I'll go work on lunch," she said. "Holler if you need me. Jake, you're okay?"

"Fine," Jake said, giving Grace one of his fingers to hold on to. "I've got her."

Lark left them alone. "She's perfect," Skye told Jake. "I mean—just look at her little hands!" She offered a finger and Grace grabbed it in her other hand. "Hi, sweetie," she said again.

Grace was apparently testing out her facial muscles because she kept opening her eyes up wide and wrinkling her forehead up and stretching out her mouth. She was, hands down, the cutest baby Skye had ever seen.

"You did such an amazing job, Skye," Jake said in a quiet whisper.

"But I haven't done *anything* yet. I haven't even fed her."

"You *made* her, babe. You're amazing," he said and she heard the waver in his voice. "I'm so in awe of you. Thank you for giving me a daughter."

"Oh, Jake." The tears started up again. She leaned her head against his shoulder and held hands with her daughter and decided that *this* was the happiest she'd ever been. In this perfect little moment of being a family for the first time.

Skye had no idea how much time had passed before Grace's little noises took on a different tone and she started to cry. "Lark?" Skye called out in alarm. "What's the matter?"

Lark came in carrying a bottle. "She's right on schedule. Jake, why don't you help me change her and then Skye can feed her. Sound good?"

"I'm getting the short end of this deal," he said good-naturedly. "Let's go, Grace." He picked her up and disappeared to where Skye had to assume there was a changing table.

Her daughter. Her perfect little daughter. Oh, how Skye wished she could even remember being pregnant, but it just wasn't there. Her pregnancy wasn't even a fog that slipped through her fingers—it was just the blankness of nothingness.

Why couldn't she remember it? There was something that didn't add up about the whole thing—the baby was just now catching up to her gestational age. She was as old as she'd have been if Skye hadn't been in the accident. And Jake had said that Skye didn't want to travel with him while she was pregnant…but if that was true, why was she driving back to Royal by herself? It was about a ten-hour drive. Why would she have made that trip alone?

She didn't know. She just didn't know, damn it all. And not knowing was *so* frustrating.

"Here we are, all clean for Mommy," Jake said as he rounded back into the room. Then he looked up at her. "What's wrong? Are you okay?"

"I'm—fine. Just trying to think," she replied with an apologetic smile.

He gave her a long look. "Are you up to feeding her?"

Lark came in behind him. "Let me get a pillow for your arm." Lark got Skye all tucked in. Jake put Grace back in her arms and all of her frustrated worries disappeared again.

She knew that she'd wanted this—a child. A family. And not just Grace and Jake, but the bigger family—Lark and Keaton and the Holts, too.

Except there was still something missing.

"Have you talked to Mom and Dad? Did they say if they were going to come by?" Skye asked Lark as Grace drank her milk.

"Ah…well—see, they've been busy. Recovering from the storm." Lark must have seen the look of alarm on Skye's face. "Just a lot of property damage. They were fine and the house was okay. Dad's just busy. Well, you know how they are."

Skye dropped her gaze back to Grace. Were her parents too busy to see her? To see Grace? David and Gloria had taken all those pictures on their phones—it was clear that they'd spent a great deal of time with Grace. "Lark—that reminds me, Gloria said to take pictures."

So Jake came back and sat beside Skye and Lark

took several photos and then emailed one to the Holts and to Keaton. "He's out on at the ranch with the dog," Lark explained.

Skye decided she wasn't going to worry anymore. Jake had said what mattered now was what happened next—Skye getting stronger, Grace getting stronger. All of them getting under the same roof. That's what she had to focus on, not what her faulty mind couldn't reconstruct.

So she studied her daughter as she ate and then watched as Jake burped the baby and ate the lunch her sister made.

Jake and Lark had clearly been making plans while they were getting Grace changed, because Jake said, "I've got to do a work thing on Friday night, Skye. I'll bring you over here and you can play with Grace."

"Okay," she quickly agreed. "I can handle lying on the floor," she added in a joking tone.

"Perfect," Lark said, looking mischievous. "It's a date."

# Nine

Friday night didn't come fast enough. Jake had taken Skye over to Lark's once a day for the afternoon feeding and playtime, which was nice, but it always felt as if the visits were too short. Skye was looking forward to spending the evening with Grace.

Finally, the appointed time arrived and Jake drove her over. Skye was surprised when Keaton answered the door. A part of her wanted to recoil the way she'd always done when they were kids. Keaton hadn't ever liked her very much.

But he gave her a warm smile and said, "Skye, good to see you up."

"Thanks," she said. New feelings crowded out

the old shame at being caught by Keaton. "How's Grace today?"

"Fussy," he admitted. "Rough night last night."

Skye's heart began to beat out a worried tempo. "Is she okay?"

"Fine," he hurried to assure her. "Babies cry. Come on in."

Skye was aware that today, she was able to make her way back to Lark's overstuffed living room without Jake having to hold her up. As much as she hated the exercises, they were working. She still used Jake as backup when she went up and down stairs, but she could now do short distances by herself.

Lark was standing in the living room, wearing a skirt and a jacket. She'd fixed her hair and was even wearing makeup. Instantly, every single one of Skye's warning bells went off. Lark had never been one to get all dressed up unless she had a good reason—and Skye was positive that a girls' night in with a three-month-old was not a good reason.

"Hi!" Lark said in a too-perky voice. "You should change. Here," she said, thrusting a garment bag into Skye's hands.

"I'm almost afraid to ask." Skye opened the bag up and tried to make sense of the light-colored fabric inside. "Is this...a cream-colored linen pantsuit?"

"Indeed it is," Lark said, trying not to giggle. "Just what all the mothers of babies are wearing this season. It's something Mom gave me a while back."

"At least it's not a pageant dress," Jake said.

"I have to wear this? *Really?*"

"Um..."

"Lark," Skye said severely. "Why on God's green earth would I need to wear a pantsuit to play with my baby?"

"You better tell her," Jake said, taking her hand and stroking her palm, as if that would calm her down.

"I have a surprise for you. Jake's going to stay with Keaton and Grace and we're going out. Our mother would have a heart attack if she saw you out in public in yoga pants. Now," she said, holding up her hand and cutting Skye off before she could protest, "go get changed. We've got to get moving."

Skye changed, a sinking pit of anxiety in her

stomach. At least she'd put on makeup after her shower with Jake today. And—she looked in the mirror—yes, her hair was passable.

But she'd been looking forward to spending time with Grace all day long. If she wasn't going to get to do that now, why hadn't Jake brought her over earlier?

And what had Lark meant about their mother? Maybe, Skye began to hope, she was going to go see her parents. The five days without so much as a peep from them had not gone unnoticed. Gloria and David had stopped by one more time and Skye had been over to Lark's every day.

But she hadn't seen her parents yet. And she didn't know why.

That must be what was going to change—yes, it seemed right, especially if Jake and Keaton were going to stay here. Okay, this made sense, Skye decided. She and Lark were probably going out to dinner with Vera and Tyrone Taylor.

She hadn't seen her parents in…in…well, since the night before she and Jake had run away, obviously. She hoped they weren't still mad at her. How could they be? The Holts had forgiven Skye and Jake. Surely the Taylors had, too?

When she was dressed, she emerged from the bathroom, feeling awkward in the scratchy linen. This was not her normal attire. The yoga pants were. Back in Houston, on the mornings when Jake had to work early and she just had some freelance work to do, Skye would lounge around in her yoga pants. She'd always paused to think about what her mother would say if she saw Skye in such attire. Vera would have thrown an epic fit that her beautiful, model-perfect daughter would dare play down her features. All the more reason for Skye to own several pairs of yoga pants.

Lark was waiting for her. "Ready?"

"I guess so?" Skye said as she kissed Grace on the top of her little head. Then she kissed Jake, although that felt weird, with both Keaton and Lark watching them. "Wish me luck."

He grinned at her. "You'll have fun," he promised. She gave him a look. It might be good to see her parents again, but that didn't necessarily mean it was going to be "fun." Vera and Tyrone Taylor were many things, but that wasn't one of them.

They headed out. Skye's legs felt pretty decent, actually. That was a good sign for tonight. Skye settled into Lark's car. The silence was almost too much for her. There was so much she'd missed— and not just from being asleep for four months. She'd missed more than four years of her sister's life. "Was Mom unbearable while I was away?"

"Oh, God," Lark said with a weary sigh. "I mean, I was always jealous that you were so beautiful and the favorite but…" She shrugged. "I didn't realize how much Mom and Dad focused on you until you weren't there. Then, suddenly, they were criticizing my every move. My every outfit," she corrected.

Skye winced. "I didn't mean to abandon you to them. Not entirely. I was pretty mad at you, wasn't I?"

"Furious," Lark agreed. But she didn't sound angry about it, or even that bitter. "I was…well, I was not kind about you and Jake. I was trying so hard to be the perfect Taylor daughter— so that Mom and Dad would care about me like they cared about you."

Skye snorted. "I don't know if I'd describe trying to force me into beauty pageants as 'caring.'" Lark gave her a look. "But I understand what you're saying."

"You were the favorite," Lark repeated. "I could

do nothing right. And I couldn't believe that you would just *throw* that away."

"But I had to," Skye said. "I love Jake. I had to be with him."

"I know. I guess that was the other reason I said what I said to you. You were going off to be happy and I...I wasn't brave enough to go get what I wanted. I was afraid."

"Lark..." Skye reached over and put her hand on her sister's shoulder.

"It's okay," Lark said, shooting her a smile. "You just knew what you wanted earlier than I did."

"You and Keaton, huh?"

"Me and Keaton. I should have listened to you all those years ago when you tried to tell me there was something about a Holt."

The two of them laughed. "I told you so," Skye said.

"You were right. Can I tell you something?"

"Sure. Anything." Skye relaxed a little bit. She couldn't fix whatever might be wrong between her and Jake right now, but being like this with Lark was a gift in and of itself. It was good to have her sister back again.

"Keaton and I are trying to have a baby."

"What? But…you're not even married yet!" She thought. She was pretty sure. She looked at Lark's hand, which just had a diamond ring on it. Not a wedding band.

Of course, she didn't have her wedding band on, either, and that didn't mean she and Jake weren't married.

"I know," Lark said with a nervous grin. "I don't know if I've ever been so happy as when it was him and me and Grace. I felt like—like that was who I was supposed to be. I can be a better mother than our mother is." She gave Skye a warm glance. "Does that shock you?"

"No, no…"

"And I know it sounds silly, but maybe another grandbaby would help heal the rift between our families, you know? You've seen how much Grace has won over Keaton's folks."

"It doesn't sound silly at all," Skye admitted. "I always thought the same thing." She sighed. "But there's so much I lost. I have this feeling I'm missing something—something *huge*—and I don't know what it is."

"Are you sure it's not a baby? Because I found her," Lark said with a laugh.

"Ha ha. Very funny. Are you going to tell me where we're going?"

"Soon," Lark replied. "I know the doctor said you might get your memory back, you might not. But you were happy, weren't you?"

"We are happy," Skye agreed. She looked out the window. The surroundings looked…familiar. "Where are we?"

"It won't take long," Lark said with obvious glee in her voice.

Skye doubted that statement. "This isn't going to be some sort of party, is it?"

"No," Lark said way too quickly. "Why do you ask?"

*"Lark,"* Skye groaned.

"Oh, look! We're here!" Lark said as she turned into the Texas Cattleman's Club.

Skye managed not to say something snarky and juvenile as she groaned. Again. "Is there anything I can do to convince you to take me home? Bribery, maybe?" Because Skye didn't have "polite and social" in her tonight. She just *didn't*. Plus, she did not want to be wearing this damn cream-colored linen suit. It was half a size too small and itched.

"I want to show you the new childcare center they added last year," Lark said in a too-bright tone. "When Grace gets stronger, you can bring her here."

"And I had to wear a linen pantsuit for that, huh?"

"Come on." Lark all but dragged her out of the car and into the TCC. Skye hadn't really been in here. She'd come for dinners with her parents, but the TCC was an old boy's club in every possible sense of the word. Her father was a long-time member.

Lark led Skye into what was unmistakably a childcare center. Toy stations and rainbow colors decorated a room with pint-size tables and chairs. "Wow, when did *this* happen?"

"Last year. After they started admitting women," Lark said.

"Wait—they admit women now? How long was I gone?"

Lark smirked. "Pretty long. Come on." She led Skye down a long hall. "Check this out," she said in that too-bright tone again. She opened the door and basically shoved Skye through it.

"Surprise!" a crowd of women all shouted together. And it was quite a crowd. Gloria Holt was there, along with Julie Kingston and a few other people Skye recognized from the hospital.

"It's your baby shower," Gloria said, grinning from ear to ear as she led Skye to a chair at the front of the room. "Well, baby shower and wel-come-home party."

Skye took in all the people. She saw Megan Maguire. "Goodness, you look wonderful, Skye! Did Jake fix your hair?"

Skye's cheeks colored. "He's getting better."

Megan grinned. "He gets any better, and I'm going to hire him to groom dogs!"

Julie Kingston came up to them. Skye almost didn't recognize her, since she was wearing a nice outfit instead of scrubs. "Hi, Julie," Skye said, putting on a nice smile.

"Hey, you remember my name! That's great," Julie said. "How are you doing?"

"Better. I've been able to spend some time with Grace—Lark's still taking care of her," Skye said. "But it turns out that I'm currently perfectly suited to lie on the floor and play with a baby."

Julie nodded knowingly. "I'm so glad you've got

Lark. She's a great nurse." Lark blushed under the weight of the compliment.

"We'll have to get together soon, maybe for coffee?" That'd be good, Skye decided. She could slowly ease back into the Royal, Texas, social circle one coffee date at a time.

Julie paused. "Oh. Well, I'm actually not sure how much longer I'm going to be here."

"What?" Lark asked, sounding truly shocked. "But you're terrific at your job and…I really like working with you. I'd hate to lose your friendship."

Julie gave Lark a weak smile. "I know, Lark. But…well, things change. We'd still be friends, though—just because I'm somewhere else doesn't mean we can't keep in touch. I just don't know how I'm going to break it to Lucas." When Skye blinked at her, she added, "Dr. Wakefield."

"Well," Lark said, "if there's anything I can do to help, just let me know."

"Thanks, I will. Now if you'll excuse me." Julie went over to the punch bowl and seemed to study it.

"Skye," Lark said, leading a slender woman with brown hair over to where Skye sat, "this is

Stella Daniels, our acting mayor. She's done an amazing job getting this town back on its feet."

"It's such a pleasure to meet you, Skye," Stella said, giving her a politician's handshake. "We can't tell you how glad we are that you're on the road to recovery. I couldn't help but feel that your fate and the town's fate were intertwined. If you can come back from that storm, so can Royal!"

A handful of other women applauded.

"Thank you," Skye said, feeling more than a little awkward. She tried to grin, but the noise in the room was much louder than she was used to and everyone was looking at her.

"Let's open the presents," Gloria announced. She was clearly having the time of her life, showing pictures of Grace to anyone who'd stand still long enough to look at them. "Then we have cake and punch!"

"Um…" Skye said. Presents? She realized that this must be how Lark had always felt—the focus of attention, but unsure of what to do or say.

And where was her mother? Surely Vera Taylor would come to her own daughter's baby shower.

Wouldn't she?

Skye took a breath, hoping the throbbing in her

head would ease. Maybe her mother was just...
running late or something. And in the meantime,
Skye was here with all these wonderful women
who'd gone to so much trouble to throw her a
party. She could do this. And once she did it,
she could go home. So she dug deep for her old-
fashioned manners. "Thank you so much, everyone," she said. "This is such a thoughtful gesture.
We can't thank you enough for everything you've
done for us."

The guests beamed, so she figured that was the
right thing to say. Lark started piling beautifully
wrapped presents onto her lap and Gloria sat next
to her, dutifully recording every gift and giver in
order.

And once Skye got going, it was actually fun.
She hadn't done a single thing to get ready for
Grace. The cute little onesies, the adorable blan-
kets—even the diaper cake was new and precious.
Skye let herself get swept up in the excitement,
*oohing* and *aahing* over every darling outfit.

This was what she'd wanted. The little swim-
mer diapers? She wanted to take Grace to a pool
this summer and splash in the water with her. The
adorable sun hats and sunglasses? Perfect for play-

ing in the yard. And the stroller? Walking would be good for both of them. She could see it now—Grace bundled up in the cute dresses, strapped into the stroller with her hat on, Jake and Skye taking turns pushing her as they walked.

There was so much she wanted to do with her baby—things that she had forgotten, along with everything else. But for the first time, it began to feel like it was possible.

A couple of times, the door opened and an older man would stick his head in, see the mass of women and baby things, and back out of the room pretty quickly. "Some of the older members haven't adjusted to women being allowed into the club," Stella explained.

"When's that going to change?" Megan wanted to know.

"Well," Stella said, standing. "This is as good a time as any to announce that I've just been asked to be a member of the TCC." The group burst into applause. "I'll be inducted along with Colby Richardson. He's already a member of the Dallas branch but this makes his Royal membership official." She positively beamed. "Aaron—that's Aaron Nichols, my fiancé," she explained to Skye.

"Aaron and I will be staying in Royal. He's going to open a branch office of his company."

"How wonderful, Stella!" Gloria said. "Does that mean you'll stay on as mayor?"

Stella grinned. "At least until the next election!"

Everyone laughed in a good-natured way. But then Paige Richardson said, "Actually, I think Colby will be returning to Dallas soon."

Megan gasped. "Oh, Paige—really?"

Paige dropped her gaze. "He's been such a big help," she admitted. "But…he's got a business to run…"

Skye was confused. Was Paige talking about her husband leaving town? No, wait—had there been two Richardson boys? They'd been older than she was. She couldn't remember.

Then Gloria cut the cake and Lark passed out slices and the group fell back into easy conversation. As exhausted as she was, Skye was glad she'd come. Yes, she was tired and yes, she couldn't wait to burn this pantsuit, but this was a community of people who were there when you needed them. She and Jake had left this behind and had been on their own for years, which had been exhilarating but also…scary. There'd been no one to fall back on when the going got rough.

This was better. Warm, comfortable. Maybe she and Jake would stay. This was the kind of place to raise a family—and raise them right. No more Taylor/Holt feuding.

The moment the thought crossed her mind, the door opened again.

"What is this?" a voice boomed and Tyrone Taylor walked into the room, his wife trailing behind him.

The room fell silent. "Ladies, this is the Texas Cattleman's Club, not a…"

Then he saw Skye, a plate of cake balanced on her knee and baby things in a pile next to her. "Oh," Tyrone said, all the wind taken right out of his sails. "There's my girl," he added in an even louder voice.

"Mom! Dad! I didn't think…" Lark went to greet her parents. She seemed to realize that the whole room was listening.

"Yes," Vera said, giving Lark air kisses on her cheeks. "We just finished dinner and…thought we'd drop by." She leaned back and appraised Lark's outfit, then sighed wearily. "I suppose that's better than those horrid scrubs you wear…" she said with a dismissive flick of her wrist.

Then she headed for Skye. "Did you have a lovely party, dear?" She stroked Skye's hair. "Where is your ring? I assumed you'd married that Holt boy."

"I did. We *are* married," Skye said, her cheeks getting hot. That Holt boy? "His name is Jake."

"Mom, Skye lost the ring in the storm," Lark said quickly.

"And he hasn't gotten you another one?" Vera *tsked* several times. "I see you at least had the good sense to wear that pantsuit." The room was quieter than church on Sunday. "Next week, we'll go shopping for some proper things," Vera went on. She leaned down, her voice dropping to an almost whisper. "I'm sure we can find something that suits your figure *somewhere*."

"That's quite enough of that, Vera," Gloria said, bustling up. "Cake?" she asked, thrusting out a plate of cake with pink frosting.

"Heavens, no. Don't you know what that will do to a figure? Well," Vera simpered, giving Gloria a cutting look, "I guess you would."

The silence was so sharp it could have cut glass.

"Ah," Tyrone said. "We'll let you get back to your little party. You take care, sweetie." He winked at Skye.

Humiliation burned her cheeks. *Too little, too late*, she thought. "Yeah, okay. Thanks for stopping in," she forced herself to say as if the plan all along had been for her parents to show up and belittle the entire baby shower.

After they showed themselves out, the women stood around in awkward silence. There were no more gifts to open, and no one seemed to be in the mood for seconds of cake.

"Well," Lark announced, "I think I need to get Skye home."

That was enough to get Julie and the nurses talking about how Skye needed to be sure not to overdo it in these first days home. Soon enough, Skye was back in Lark's car, a plate of cake for Jake in her lap. Gloria had promised to load up all the baby things, wash everything and deliver it all tomorrow afternoon, along with the typed list of gifts. Skye gathered that was part of making sure she didn't overdo it.

When they were safely in the car, Skye asked, "Were Mom and Dad always that bad?"

Lark sighed. "No, not to you. To me, yeah."

"God, and I never caught on." Skye felt stupid.

Lark shook her head. "Mom can be very subtle when she wants. When we were growing up, I think you looked so much like she used to that at first she liked you better, but then…" She shrugged. "Sometimes it feels like she's competing with you. She doesn't do that with me. But I guess it's because she thinks I'm such a lost cause it's no competition to begin with."

Skye gaped at her sister. "Really? That—that makes a *lot* of sense, actually." It would explain that victorious grin at seeing Skye in this stupid pantsuit. "I thought—when you made me put this thing on—I thought we were going out to dinner with them."

"They…they had plans, Skye. But they were able to stop by."

"You're making excuses for them," she told Lark. "Don't do that. They were horrible tonight and we both know it. What I want to know is, did they come see me when I was in the hospital? Gloria said she read to me."

"She did. But Mom and Dad…they came once.

I think it upset Dad to see you like that, so they stayed away."

They hadn't come. They hadn't sat by her bedside and talked to her or read her books or done a single thing that might have made her feel better. "What about Grace? Gloria and David had all these pictures of her. Did Mom and Dad see her? Did they hold her?"

"They…" Lark sighed. "Okay, I don't want to upset you, but when we had Grace tested and the results showed she was Jake's daughter, they… they didn't seem to want to have anything to do with her."

"With me," Skye added. She supposed this wasn't a shock, none of it. Vera had never been the warm, loving kind of woman who held fun baby showers and went out of her way to get groceries. And Tyrone refused to have anything to do with the Holts.

Still, Skye was their daughter. And Grace? Their only granddaughter—at least for now.

Maybe her family never would accept her, not as long as she was married to Jake.

Which reminded her. "Lark, do you have any of my jewelry?"

"Oh! Yes," Lark said, clearly relieved to have something else to talk about besides their parents. "Well, sort of. You had earrings in, but the side that hit the car—that stone is gone. So I have a diamond of yours."

"Not a ring?" She'd never taken it off, not once since they'd married. "Not my wedding ring?"

"No," Lark said apologetically. "I'm sorry. Either the wind took it or…" There she paused, so unexpectedly that Skye's head popped up and she stared at her sister. "Well," Lark said hastily, "there really isn't an *either/or*, is there? It was lost in the tornado."

There it was again, that feeling that there was *something* that Skye should know and simply didn't. "What aren't you telling me?"

"Nothing," Lark answered quickly. "We're home. Do you want to come in and say good night to Grace?"

Skye sighed. "Yes," she said, but she wasn't happy that Lark was holding out on her.

Just like she thought Jake was sometimes holding out on her, too. They both acted as if something had happened that Skye couldn't recall and she shouldn't be allowed to know what it was. It was infuriating.

But—was she really mad at Lark and Jake? Or was she just mad? After all, her parents had treated her like crap tonight. Wasn't she still mad at them? They were having dinner—alone—in the same building where the baby shower was. How were those "plans" more important than seeing their daughter?

Okay, fine. Skye was just mad. She was probably tired, too—it'd been a long day.

She'd go inside and kiss her daughter and have her husband take her home.

But tomorrow, she wanted some answers.

# Ten

"How are things going with Skye?" Keaton was standing in the doorway of the living room, a towel slung over his shoulder.

Jake looked up at his brother from where he lay on the floor, next to Grace. The baby was on her tummy, making those weird grunting noises. Jake had been giving her pep talks on lifting her head up, but so far, no progress.

"Fine," he said. He was still having trouble reconciling the Keaton before him with the Keaton who'd tried to undermine him for years. "I hope she's having fun at that baby shower."

"She remember anything?"

That's what Keaton said. What he meant was,

had Skye remembered not telling Jake she was pregnant—or why?

Jake would not fly off the handle at his brother. The man had changed, after all—caring for Jake's daughter, building a house for Skye's sister—definitely not anything Jake would have ever figured him for. Maybe things could be different now. Better, even.

But Jake still didn't know how to trust his own brother. So he said, "Not much. I'm hoping that no one says or does anything at the shower to upset her tonight. We've been focused on her physical rehab for now."

Keaton snickered. "I bet you have."

"Watch it," Jake snapped.

Keaton held his hands up in surrender. "Easy, man, easy. Whatever you're doing, it's working. She looks a hell of a lot better than she did in that hospital."

That was good. Truth be told, they were having a lot of sex—the kind of sex they'd had in the first year or so of their marriage. And it did seem to be making Skye very happy. Jake wasn't complaining, either. "She wants Grace to come home with us," Jake admitted.

"Yeah?" Keaton thought about this for a while. "Home, where? You going to take them both back to Houston?"

All in all, it was probably the most diplomatic way of asking the same question Keaton had asked when Jake had first met his daughter—*you going to slip off into the night with your baby*?

And truthfully? Jake wanted to. Yeah, his parents were being great and yeah, Keaton hadn't stabbed him in the back or anything, but that didn't mean that Jake didn't see the ghosts of events past everywhere he looked.

He wanted to go back to being in charge of his own life again.

"I'm not sure. I actually have a meeting about the next job Monday afternoon—an internet video interview. I planned on bringing Skye over here so she could play with Grace."

"Another year in Bahrain or wherever?" There was no missing the judgment in Keaton's voice.

"North America. Three weeks on, one week off. In my line of work, that's a really cushy schedule." He could probably do one week a month in Royal. It wouldn't be as if he lived here, after all. It would just be…a vacation house where his wife and child lived. And Skye would be happier if she stayed here, he knew. Even she remembered wanting to come home. She just didn't remember telling him about it.

Jake held up his finger and grinned as Grace did her level best to clamp down on it. "You're already pretty strong, aren't you?"

Grace sighed.

God, this little girl pulled at him in ways he'd never imagined possible. She'd only been a part of his life for a week and already he was having trouble remembering what it'd been like before.

Three weeks on, one week off—was that something he could really do? Go three weeks without seeing Grace?

Hell, could he go that long without *Skye*? Yeah, he'd spent ten months away from her, but that had been when things were bad between them. Right now, that seemed like such a distant memory as to have been another life. Right now, she was the woman he'd always loved. The woman he always wanted to love.

He didn't know. He just didn't know.

Keaton was staring at him. Jake got the feeling his big brother wanted to say something—several somethings—and none of them would be complimentary.

So Jake decided to change the subject.

"Mom said the tornado turned up the original land deed in town hall?" The Holt family had long claimed the Taylors had stolen part of the Holts' land—and the Taylors had always claimed the Holts were on their property. Neither side had proof. The land deeds had long been lost.

Keaton nodded. He went to a drawer and pulled out a piece of paper that had been folded over and over. "The original is with our lawyers," he said as he unfolded the copy. The deed took up almost half of the dining-room table.

Jake picked up Grace. Even if Lark had said it was okay to leave the baby on the ground, he still didn't like it. It just felt wrong. Plus, Keaton's dog was right over there. Jake didn't want to leave Grace where the dog could get her.

Keaton was unfolding a second sheet of paper—a map. "This is the current fence line," he said, pointing to an ugly red line down the middle. "And according to the deed, this," he said, pointing to a blue line almost three inches away, "is the original property line."

"What's the scale?" Jake said, rubbing Grace's back.

"One inch equals one thousand feet."

Jake whistled, which caused Grace to start. "Sorry, sweetie," he said. "That's close to a half mile."

"Actually, you figure in how long the fence runs, it comes out to almost two thousand acres."

"*Damn*. Dang," Jake quickly corrected. There was a child in the room.

"I could use the land," Keaton told him. "The ranch's finances are still struggling from the tornado. More land means more cattle and better grazing. There are several small lakes and a spring on what they claim is their land that would make a big difference in how many cattle I can support. Hell, the value of the land alone is close to two million."

"What's it going to take, then?" Jake asked. "To get the Taylors to admit they're in the wrong?"

"Don't know," Keaton said. "If we only had some independent proof—so that Tyrone can't claim I forged it…" He shook his head. "I tried, you know. I went out there to make peace, for Lark. Told him I wanted to marry his daughter and maybe we could just let bygones be bygones."

"How'd that work out for you?"

"Oh, you know—the usual. He accused me of forging the documents. And they've basically disowned Lark."

Independent proof. That's what Jake needed. Irrefutable evidence that Skye's great-great-great-grandfather or whoever had moved the line and misappropriated Holt land.

How the hell was Jake supposed to get that?

Keaton sighed. "It's not all bad. Tyrone's stuck. He can't sell the land without a bill of sale and we will sue him if he 'finds' one. And if he can't get rid of the land, it'll be handed down to Lark and Skye, just like our land will go to us. We just have to wait him out."

"Great. Another generation of waiting. Yippee."

Keaton snorted as he pointed to a black square that almost sat on the red line. "I'm not waiting. I'm building Lark a house. Mom and Dad offered to let us have the ranch house when they retire to Gulf Shores, but…I wanted her to have someplace that was her own. It's going to have a gourmet kitchen and a library for all of her books and plenty of room. She says maybe we'll have three or four kids." Keaton laughed. "Can you imagine? Me and Lark with four kids all running around."

Actually, Jake was having a lot of trouble imagining that. "Which side of the fence are you building?" he asked, eyeing the map.

"The Holt side—but," Keaton said with a mean grin, "man, it's snugged up against that fence line. You could walk out of the house and cross over into what Tyrone claims is 'his' land. You know, you could take over the ranch house after Mom and Dad move out. We'd be neighbors."

Jake could. He could go back home and erase all the bad memories of the past, the same way he was trying to do with Skye now. He could put his family in his childhood home and just…

Pretend nothing had happened? Wasn't he already doing that? He was hanging out with Keaton, as if the man had never betrayed him. He was taking care of Skye, as if the past two years had been nothing but a lousy dream after too many burritos.

Could he do that forever?

What about when she remembered? Would she

still want him? And would she go on pretending that the divorce papers had been a figment of his imagination—or not?

When they'd first run off, they'd gotten a one-bedroom apartment and set up their computers on a rickety table they'd bought at a thrift store. They'd lived cheaply and worked from home, him on building his IT business, her on her graphic design business. They'd spent most of the day—and the night—together. If the mood hit them, Jake would pull her out of her chair and take her to bed. And when the bed was too far away, he'd take her to the couch.

It'd just been them against the world for about eight months. Him and Skye, like it was supposed to be.

Then his business had started to take off. He'd won a couple of bids, got some good references and begun taking more jobs. He'd been home less and less, although Skye still worked from home. They'd moved into a better place after one lucrative job, gotten nicer things. They'd left the rickety table behind.

There'd been a time when that…hadn't worked as well. They'd had better stuff—nicer cars, better clothes and a much nicer place—but Jake had been working insane hours. He hadn't been home as much. He'd missed her, but he hadn't been able to back off from the job. Texas Sky Consulting had been taking off and a secure financial future that was completely independent of either of their families was no small thing.

When international clients had started inquiring about Jake's services, he'd asked Skye to come with him. They'd jetted around the world together and on those trips, they'd gotten a taste of the closeness that had marked their first year together. Yeah, Jake still worked, but Skye was included in dinners and parties. And since neither of them spoke anything besides English and a little Spanish, they stuck together even more.

But then…then they'd gone back home. He'd gone back to work. And left Skye alone.

To see the love in her eyes dim a little more every day.

As Jake patted Grace's back, he remembered how he'd felt during those times. There was a wall between them, things left unsaid. He hadn't liked it then and he didn't like it now.

The fact of the matter was, he'd put his business before Skye. He'd convinced himself he was doing it for her—providing for their future to-gether—but was that really reason enough to work seventy-hour weeks? To go days without touching her?

*Weeks* without touching her?

"Mom has offered," he told Keaton. "I'm thinking about it. It'd make Skye happy to stay here."

"Yeah? Would it make you happy?"

Jake gritted his teeth. *Not yet it wouldn't*, he thought—but he kept that to himself. Luckily, Grace started to fuss. "Is it bedtime?" Jake asked, looking at the clock.

"Yup. Let me get her bottle. You want to do this on your own?"

"Yeah," Jake said. He got why Skye was always saying she wanted to care for the baby herself. There was something sweet about being the one to feed and burp—and yes, even change the diapers.

As he fed and rocked Grace until she fell asleep, Jake realized that he didn't know much, but he knew that he loved Skye and that he loved Grace.

He'd almost lost his family once.

He'd do anything to hold on to them.

* * *

*"Oh,"* Skye whispered when she saw Jake rocking Grace to sleep. "Hi."

Jake smiled up at her—the picture of a doting father. Skye was filled with love. She'd wanted this—something told her she'd known this was what would happen. A baby would solve so many of the things that had driven her and Jake away from Royal in the first place.

And Grace had. Skye was close to Lark again. By all appearances, Jake and Keaton had spent an evening together without killing each other. And Gloria was going to wash all the baby things and bring them over to help Skye get the house ready for when Grace could come home.

Grace just hadn't worked her charm on Tyrone and Vera Taylor.

Jake held up his hand, as if to say, *Just a minute*. He carefully got up and laid the baby down in her crib.

Skye joined him, leaning against his shoulder as they watched their daughter sleep. Grace was perfect—getting stronger every day, too. Just like Skye.

Jake leaned down and kissed her lightly. "Ready to go home?"

"Do we have to?" Skye knew the answer to that, but still, she wanted to stay with Grace.

"We'll come back tomorrow," he promised her. Then he kissed her again. "I'll make it worth your while."

She grinned and took his arm. After the semi-disastrous baby shower, she wouldn't mind falling asleep in Jake's arms. "Good night, my little bit of Grace." She leaned down and tenderly ran her hand over her little girl's head. "Sleep well."

Lark was waiting for them downstairs. "I have to work tomorrow, so it'll just be Keaton," she told them. "Oh, and Skye—here's your diamond."

"What?" Jake said. "What diamond?"

"My one earring," Skye said, handing him the little bag with one earring and a post in it. "Lark said they didn't find the other diamond or my wedding ring."

The blood drained out of Jake's face. "Oh. Well. I'll…hang on to this for you, okay?"

They said their goodbyes to Keaton and Lark and then Jake took her home. "I wish I had my ring," she told him in the car. Exhausted, she slumped against the window, watching the brownness that was Texas in February slide past. "You should have seen the look my mother gave me tonight. It made me almost feel like we weren't married anymore."

He made a choking noise. "We are, babe. We are still married."

*Still.*

What a strange word.

She looked at him. His wedding ring glinted in the light of the dash. Still. *Still.*

Something wasn't right.

She closed her eyes and tried to think—but no, she was too danged tired to come up with the echo of something Jake might have said once—*why do you* still *want to go back there*?

*Why aren't I enough for you?*

Skye jolted straight up in her seat. What the heck was that? She looked at Jake.

"What? What?" he repeated. "Are you okay?" He looked over at her. "You can't let your mom get to you, babe. I never really understood why you wanted to come back here, to be closer to that."

"I just…" She sighed. She didn't remember discussing this with him, but on the other hand, the conversation had a familiar feel to it. "I wanted things to be different. Better."

Jake was silent after that, which left Skye feeling kind of hopeless and she wasn't even sure why. After all, things were better. Lark and Keaton, Gloria and David—those relationships were one-hundred-percent better now than when Jake and Skye had slipped off into the night four years ago.

She was too tired to think—and definitely too tired to be reading something into Jake's nonresponse. They were almost home anyway.

He pulled into the drive and shut the car off, but he didn't get out right away.

"Jake?" Had she crossed some line she didn't remember she shouldn't cross?

"It's nothing," he said. "I bet you're beat. Let's get you to bed."

Even though Skye's legs were getting stronger, Jake scooped her out of her seat and carried her into the house. She let him. She rested her head on his shoulder as he carried her up the stairs. Then he went back down to lock up while she used the bathroom. She got into bed and a few minutes later, he climbed in with her.

He pulled her into a tight embrace, but it wasn't an erotic touch. He clung to her as if he were afraid she'd be blown away with the next strong wind that roared through.

"Skye," he said in such a serious voice that a pit of nerves opened up in her stomach.

"What is it?" Because there had to be an *it*—a something that she didn't know but should.

He laced his fingers with hers and held them over her heart. "I wanted things to be better, too."

She let those words sift through her mind. He could be talking about their parents or her accident or Grace being a preemie or any number of things.

But she didn't think he was. She thought he was talking about the two of them.

"Are we…are we okay?"

When he didn't answer immediately, the nerves kicked straight over to stark panic. She didn't know if she was going to cry or not.

"We are," he said, but he didn't sound convinced. "I have loved you for twenty years, Skye. Nothing—*nothing*—has ever changed that. And nothing ever will. You know that, right?"

"I do," she said, her voice shaking. "You know I love you too, right?"

He lifted up her left hand and kissed her bare

ring finger. "I just…I don't want you to forget that, that's all."

"I couldn't, Jake. I couldn't—not you."

He rolled into her, saying, "Don't," as he kissed her. "Don't forget this, my blue-eyed Skye."

"I won't," she promised him as their bodies joined again and again. "I will always remember you, Jake."

# Eleven

*Why aren't I enough for you?* Skye looked around, but she couldn't see where Jake was. His voice just *was*.

*You were—when you were here*, she said back—or thought back—or however they were talking.

Except they weren't talking. They were shouting. They were fighting. And Jake…Jake walked away? From her?

She jolted awake, her heart pounding as she gasped for air. Was that real? Had that happened? Or had it been a dream? No, not a dream—a nightmare.

It had to be a nightmare because Jake was lying in bed next to her. He'd sworn he loved her and then made love to her, and she was safe in his arms. They were home in Royal and they would go see Grace tomorrow and…

Except for one thing. She could still see the scene. Their apartment in Houston, her standing at the window, Jake packing up a bag and saying, "I already signed the contract." He'd made no move toward Skye—made no attempt to comfort her. "I leave in two weeks."

She pinched her arm, which hurt. She wasn't still dreaming. She was *remembering*.

"So it's settled, then," she'd said to him. God, she remembered how the distance between them had felt impossibly huge.

Skye began to panic.

"You could still come with me." That's what he'd said. Not that he loved her, not that he couldn't live without her.

"You could still stay. We could go home together, start our family." That was what she'd said back. Not that she couldn't bear to lose him, not that he was her everything.

And he'd left. He'd left without another word.

And she'd…

Oh, God. *Oh, God.*

She'd thrown her ring out the window.

Skye began to sob.

One minute, he was asleep. The next, Skye was making horrible choking noises.

"Babe?" he said, trying to keep calm as he pulled her into his arms. "Babe, you're okay. I'm here now. I'm right here."

"Oh, Jake," she wept. "I didn't mean it. I didn't mean it."

No. God, no. Had she been— "It's okay," he soothed as he stroked her hair and her back, trying to calm her down. "What happened?"

"I—the dream."

Jake forced himself to breathe in and out. "What did you dream?"

"We had a fight. And I woke up, but it wasn't a dream, was it? It *wasn't*." It was hard to understand her through the tears.

Jake's hands stilled against her. "What—" He swallowed, trying desperately to keep his cool. "What else did you remember?" The word cut into his mouth as if he were chewing glass.

Because this was it. This was the moment he'd been dreading.

"Bahrain? But I thought you were in New York for that job. But you were going to Bahrain. For, like, a year. A year!"

Damn. She *was* remembering—sort of. Her brain was trying to put the past back in place.

"Babe," he said, rubbing her back. "It's okay, babe."

"You left. You left *me*."

He was not supposed to lie to her. He could gloss over the truth. Julie at the hospital had said so.

But how could he gloss over this? He could convince her it'd all been a bad dream, that he'd been in New York for a short time instead of another country for almost a year.

He could…he could convince her that she was wrong. He could make her think that she couldn't trust her own mind. He could make himself look like a better man—at the expense of her mental health.

No, he couldn't do that. Not to her.

Still, he tried to sidestep the heart of the matter. She was already upset—and that was something the doctors had said he needed to avoid. He didn't want to make it worse.

"I came back," he told her. "I came back for you."

She gasped again. "You—you really *did* leave me?" When he didn't answer, she demanded, "For how long?"

"Skye…"

"For how long, Jacob Holt?"

There was no way to sidestep this. His only choice was to go straight ahead. "For about ten months."

"To New York?"

"To Bahrain."

That, apparently, was too much. Suddenly, Skye was out of his arms and out of the bed. "You left me for ten months to go to *Bahrain*?"

"Skye…" he said in what he hoped was a calming voice.

"No—don't *Skye* me." She dropped her head in her hands. "Oh, God—I do remember. I remember *everything*." Then she was hurrying to the bathroom before he could get the damned covers off.

"Skye, wait!" he called as the door shut behind her. He made it to the door, but it was locked. Damn. "Skye, listen—things are different now."

"Did you even know about Grace?" came the

muffled cry from the bathroom. "Did you even know about her before you showed up here?"

"No. I didn't hear from you for months. You didn't tell me."

"Oh, God..."

"Skye," he pleaded. "I'm trying. I came back for you. I'm taking care of you. I'm renting a house in Royal, Texas, for crying out loud—and you know how much I hate this damn town. I mean, I'm even considering taking the ranch house from my folks so that you and Grace can stay here because I know that's what you want, dammit."

"But I...I threw my ring away. Did I want a divorce? Oh, God—I did, didn't I?" This was followed by more crying.

"Skye—please, babe. Yes, I came home to find divorce papers waiting for me. But that's not what I want and I've spent the last couple of weeks doing everything I can to show you that you— you and Grace—come first in my life."

He rested his head against the door. This was where he'd come to in his life—talking to a bathroom door while naked. "I wanted things to be different, too. Better. I didn't want things to end like they did. You've got to believe me, babe."

"Why didn't you tell me? Why did you let me carry on like we were still in love?"

"Because we *are* still in love," Jake insisted. "I love you. Nothing has changed that, Skye. Not divorce papers, not amnesia—not anything."

There was no response.

He tried the knob again. Still locked. He could break down the door, but somehow he didn't think that was the best way to keep her calm right now.

"I didn't tell you because the doctor told me not to upset you. He said you had to remember it on your own. Well, now you have. I'm not hiding anything from you, Skye. We have a child now. We can make this work. I love you and I love Grace. We have the family you always wanted. Don't throw that away, Skye."

"Even if I want to stay in Royal?"

Jake swallowed. What the hell. He was already living in Royal, after all. "Even if you want to stay in Royal." He heard her sniff. "Skye, come back to bed. Things will seem better in the morning, I promise."

The door opened—but just a crack. "Will you still love me? Tomorrow?"

"I will still love you *always*," he promised,

knowing the words were true. "I couldn't stop even if I tried."

She gave him a teary smile. "Okay. We'll talk tomorrow, right?"

"Absolutely. Anything you want. But come to bed now, okay? The doctor would string me up by my toes if he knew I was letting you get this upset."

She nodded and opened the door. Jake walked her to the bed and tucked her in, then slid in next to her.

They lay together in the silence for a long time. Neither of them slept.

Jake spent the next two days doing everything except throwing himself at Skye's feet and begging for forgiveness. And there were a few times when he considered that to be his best option.

Skye's memory was returning in fits and starts. "Were you in Venezuela for six months?" she asked at one point.

"Yes." This was a kind of hell, having her pass judgment on all his past sins all over again. "You came down for a few weeks, but you didn't like it there, so you came back."

Because that was all he could do right now—be completely honest about the past. It was clear that she was going to recover most, if not all, of those memories and the last thing he wanted to do was undermine her trust in him a second time.

"Right. I hated Venezuela," she replied. "Are you going to take another job like that? Like Bahrain? Where you're gone for months and months at a time?"

"No," he promised her. "I don't want to leave you or Grace for that long. That was the mistake I made last time. I won't make it again."

Every time they had a variation on this conversation, Skye would nod her head and say, "Okay," and that would be it for another hour or so, until she got another piece of the puzzle and wanted to know where it fit.

They went to see Grace. Lark was home the second day and could clearly tell that something was off, but she didn't say anything.

Desperate to avoid having their dirty laundry aired to Lark, Jake focused on Grace with a laser-like intensity. He fixed the bottles and changed the diapers and did everything he could think of to show Skye how devoted he was. When his mother showed up with all the presents that Skye had received at the baby shower, Jake even sat there and acted as interested as he could as they showed him everything. There was only so much enthusiasm he could muster for onesies, but he tried, dammit. He tried for Skye.

They hadn't made love again, but that was okay. Skye was still sleeping in bed with him and there, under the cover of darkness, she began to talk to him.

"I still feel like I'm missing things," she said. "I don't—I don't have Grace, you know? I don't remember being pregnant. I don't know if it was an easy pregnancy or a hard one or anything."

"It'll come back," he told her. "And if it doesn't, we'll have to have another baby so you can remember it."

She hugged him. "You'd have another baby with me?"

"Of course. We're a family, after all. I'm in this for the long haul, no matter what."

"Oh, Jake—I don't want a divorce," she told him. "I just want you."

"Then I'm yours."

Which was all very good and well.
Except for one thing.
He had a job interview on Monday.

# Twelve

Skye's head was still a mess—but she was starting to set things to rights again.

She'd remembered most of how it had gone bad—Jake had kept taking longer and longer jobs away from home, but he didn't want to come back to Royal. Skye remembered feeling trapped and abandoned and those memories were hard.

But they were softened by the Jake she had by her side right now—the man who helped her with her exercises and cooked her meals and played with their daughter. The man who talked about moving out into his parents' ranch home so Grace would have wide open spaces in which to grow up, just down the way from where Keaton and

Lark would live. The man who talked of having another baby, once they got Grace home and she was stronger.

Sometimes, it was hard to reconcile the two versions of Jake that were fighting for space in her head.

So, when Monday came and he said he had to do something for work and he was just going drop her off at Lark's, she did her level best not to worry about it. "You're not flying out to Siberia or anything, right?" she half joked.

"Nope. Just a phone call," he assured her as he walked in with her.

Lark wasn't there—it was just Keaton. Skye tried not to feel nervous about that—after all, this was not the same Keaton who'd never liked her or her family. This was the Keaton who loved Lark and made her happy and took care of Grace as if she were his own.

"Ready for some tummy time?" Keaton asked Skye. "I think Miss Grace is ready to play with her mommy."

"I'll be back in a couple of hours, okay?" Jake said as he kissed Grace's head. "You have fun with her," he added as he kissed Skye goodbye.

Keaton laid Grace down on the activity mat and waited patiently for Skye to get down on the ground, too. "You want some lunch?" he asked.

"Sure," she said, although as far as she could tell, Lark had been doing all the meals. She wasn't sure if Keaton could actually cook or not.

"How have you been doing?" Keaton asked from the kitchen.

"Better. I'm starting to remember things," she told him as Grace made her little grunting noise. Skye put her hand on Grace's back and felt the baby's muscles working. "You can do it, sweetie," she told the baby. "Stronger every day. Mommy has tummy time, too, you know."

Grace made a cooing noise.

"Really?" Keaton said, the surprise in his voice obvious. "You're getting stuff back?"

Skye mentally smacked herself in the head. What was she doing, telling that to Keaton? She really didn't want to have this conversation with him. If Lark were here, she might be open with her sister. But she still hadn't figured out how to interact with Keaton outside of talking about the baby. "Yes."

Keaton came to the doorway and looked down at her. "And you and Jake...you're cool?"

"Yes," she said again, trying to turn her attention back to Grace. The baby was stretching her arms out, which made her look like a Super Baby in training.

"Wow. Okay." Keaton scratched his head. "Well, that's..." He looked at her and paused. "That's great. Really glad to hear it."

There it was again, that feeling that people were holding out on her. But it wasn't as if Skye were having this conversation with Lark. This was Keaton, and she was not comfortable with him. "Yes," she said. "It's great."

She swallowed. Keaton knew something but he didn't appear to be in any hurry to tell her. Maybe she could...find something out? Because she was so tired of knowing she was missing something. She was stronger now.

"It's not like he's not going to fly to Siberia or anything," she added, doing a decent impression of calm. "I'm not worried."

Keaton's eyebrows were almost up to his hairline. "Oh, okay. So...yeah. Well, that's good."

She frowned. That was not an informative response. She picked up Grace and laid the little girl on her chest. For a moment, she forgot about trying to figure out what she didn't know because what she *knew*, right now, was that this was her little girl and together they were getting stronger. She could feel Grace's little heartbeat fluttering against hers.

But she wanted to know what she was missing because it seemed important. It was her future, wasn't it? And Jake had said the past didn't matter, not compared to what would happen in the future.

"I know he said..." She paused. "Shoot. I can't remember where he said his next job was?"

Keaton rubbed the back of his neck, looking uncomfortable. "He told you?"

"Yes, of course." She hoped it came out sounding confident. "We don't have secrets."

"Well..." Keaton sighed. "I'm glad you're okay with it. I didn't think that being gone three weeks out of the month was the best thing, but Lark and I are happy to help out when he's gone." He smiled encouragingly.

Was *that* what Jake was doing—interviewing for a job that would take him away for three weeks of the month? "Oh, yeah—that'll be great.

We're still working out the details," she said, feeling stupid.

Because they weren't working the details out at all. Jake was still putting work ahead of her—her and Grace.

No, it wasn't ten months in Bahrain or even three months in New York—but only seeing him one week out of the month? How was she supposed to take care of Grace by herself? She couldn't bear to leave Grace here at Keaton and Lark's for much longer. She'd been focused on getting stronger so they could bring Grace home—together.

Skye wanted her family, damn it. She wanted the people she loved most—Jake and Grace and the other babies they'd talked about having together—all under one roof, living side by side, day in and day out.

And what if they did have another baby? What then? Would Skye be doing the pregnancy alone— again? Would she be delivering the baby alone— *again*?

Because *why*? Because Jake was out on yet another damned job, talking about how this job would lead to bigger and better things? Things that would slowly erode at the amount of time he was home until they were going almost a year without laying eyes on each other—*again*?

Skye held Grace tight to avoid looking at Kea ton. A buzzer went off in the kitchen and he left the room.

What was she going to do now? Skye's mind raced. She had gotten most of her memory back, but she still didn't remember large chunks of the last ten months.

Jake loved her. He'd said it—shown it—time and time again.

But...

Did he love her enough to actually stay in Royal with her? Was she more important than the job?

She didn't know.

But she sure as hell was going to find out.

"Great," Carl said. "Thanks for your time today, Jake. We've been most impressed with your previous work."

Jake smiled into the web camera and tried not to notice how it distorted his grin into a bucktoothed nightmare. "If you have any other questions about how I can adapt the technology to your specific needs, just let me know."

"Great," Carl said again. He seemed to have a limited vocabulary in this regard. "We'll let you know our decision within the week."

The video call ended. By and large, the interview had gone well. Great, even, as Carl would say.

Would Jake actually take the job?

This was his company. This was what he did. And because he wanted to make sure that the job was done well, he'd always insisted on doing it himself instead of farming it out to employees. When Texas Sky did a job, the technology and production would be as promised or better.

He sat there, staring at the computer screen. In four years, he'd created a company worth millions of dollars by sheer dint of the sweat of his brow. He *was* his company and the prospect of giving up control of it—any of it—was hard for him to swallow.

But then, giving up any time with Skye and Grace was even harder for him to swallow.

He'd made this bed by insisting that he was the only one who could do his work. But did it really have to be that way?

After all, if he was the one who did everything—bid all the jobs, did all the on-site work— how much could his company grow? He'd always be doing one job at a time. Sure, the jobs paid well, but…

But what if he wanted to expand? Take on more jobs? Build his clientele?

He could hire out. He could expand now, not at some undetermined point in the future. He could do most of his work out of the office, not on-site. He could keep his company *and* keep his family.

The enormity of this realization stunned him. All he had to do was…let go.

Let go of it all. The control he insisted on having to run his business. Let go of the grudges that kept him from admitting that maybe his family had changed.

That maybe, just maybe, he'd changed.

What better way to show Skye that he had put her first than to do this for her—for them?

The more he thought about it, the better this idea seemed. There was only one hitch in the whole plan—Skye's family. Jake knew the Holts would be happy if he stayed, and Lark would, as well. But Tyrone and Vera Taylor?

Jake should try to talk to the Taylors. He didn't

have any illusion that it would go well, not after Skye's descriptions of their behavior at the baby shower. But if he could somehow smooth things out between Tyrone and Vera Taylor and Skye—well, wasn't that what Skye wanted?

Jake was on the verge of calling Tyrone Taylor when the doorbell rang. *What now?* he thought with a growl.

He threw open the door to find a deliveryman standing on the stoop. "Afternoon," he said. "Need a signature." He held out an overnight envelope addressed to Skye Taylor.

*Taylor?*

Jake signed and took the envelope. He stared at it after the delivery van had driven off. Why was Skye getting overnight packages from…?

He stared at the return address. From Matthews Private Investigations in Houston? What the hell? What did she want with a PI?

Questions swarmed around him like bees. When had she hired the PI? Why? Was she having him investigated? Or his family? Was she looking for ammo in the Taylor/Holt feud? And how had he gotten this address?

The alarm on his phone chimed—he had to go pick up Skye.

He tucked the envelope under his arm and grabbed his keys.

Only one way to find out—that was to ask her.

He could tell something was wrong from the moment he walked into Lark's house.

Oh, everything looked okay. Skye was in the recliner with a sleeping Grace against her chest. Keaton was on his laptop. Soft classical music filled the air. "Hey," he said to Keaton.

Skye didn't look at him.

"Babe," he whispered as he leaned over to kiss Grace on top of her head.

"Let's go," Skye said. "I want to go home."

"Everything okay?" He looked back at Keaton. The man wasn't acting guilty—but there was definitely something off about Skye.

"Fine," Keaton replied as he stood and came to take Grace from Skye. "I'll put her down. You guys coming back tomorrow?"

"Yes," Skye said, and again, Jake heard the stiffness in her voice.

He didn't say anything about it until they were

in the car. "You okay?" he asked without starting the engine. If he had to go in and beat the hell out of Keaton, he didn't want to leave the car running. "Everything okay with you and Keaton?"

"Oh, sure. You know, same old same old." She crossed her arms. Then, catching sight of the envelope on the dash, she asked, "What's that?"

"Actually," he replied, trying to sound calm— even though he felt nothing like calm at the moment. "I was hoping you could tell me that. It was just delivered—and it's addressed to you. From a private investigator."

He watched her as he told her this. What kind of reaction would she have? Recognition? Confusion? Desperation?

Skye cocked her head to one side and picked the envelope up. She opened it and pulled out a typed letter and an odd-looking piece of paper that had been folded many times and was in a protective plastic envelope.

She read the letter and then looked at him. "Did you do this?" she demanded, thrusting the letter at him.

"No," he said reflexively, even if he didn't know

what it was yet. "I'm not the one who hired a private eye." He took the letter and read.

*Ms. Taylor,*

*I have located the original land deed in the Texas General Land Office that shows the property line between the Taylor and Holt lands as set 114 years ago. The deed had been misfiled at some point, possibly intentionally. This deed conclusively proves that the Taylors relocated the fence line, probably at some point in the 1920s.*

*I have included a copy of the original deed for your records.*

*Please advise as to how you'd like me to proceed with the deed. I'm sure both parties involved would like to get a hold of this original. Would you like me to forward it to the Holts or the Taylors?*

*Regards,*

*Reggie Matthews, P.I.*

Jake sat there, blinking at the letter. This was it—the smoking gun that showed the Taylors had cheated the Holts out of all that land. This was what Keaton needed—independent proof of the Taylors' treachery.

But as monumental as this information was, his eyes were drawn not to the deed but to the header on the letter. Ms. Taylor. Skye had already gone back to her maiden name by the time she'd hired this guy. "You hired a PI to dig up the land deed?"

"I…must have?" Skye didn't sound sure.

"Well, you did." When she flinched, he realized it had come out harsh, but what the ever-loving hell? Here he was, doing everything to win her back and she was—what? "Who were you going to give the deed to, Skye? Your family— or mine?"

Because that was the question. Had she been working to end the feud—or looking for a way back into Tyrone and Vera Taylor's good graces?

Her face was creased in concentration as she stared at the copy in her lap. "I don't…I don't remember hiring him. I don't remember what I wanted him to do."

"You don't? Or are you just conveniently forgetting, *Ms. Taylor*?" She flinched again, but he didn't care. Here he was, ready to give up control of his company for her—and she was working against the Holts. Even if she didn't remember, she'd been willing to hurt not just him, but his family. "You were going to go back to your parents, weren't you? You always wanted to come home. You said so all the time."

Something in her seemed to snap and her confusion disappeared. "Oh, and I suppose you were going to take that job without even telling me? How did your interview go—the one where you're going to be gone three weeks out of the month?"

Jake froze. "What?"

"You had an interview for a job that's three weeks on and one week off, right? Or did you forget to tell me that?"

"What? How did you—Keaton." Damn it all to hell, that man would always, *always* stab Jake in the back.

"Yes, Keaton. I told him I was getting things back and he asked me how we were going to deal with this job you wanted. Jake, I thought you…" Here her voice broke. "I thought you were going to stay with me. I thought we were going to be a family. Because you loved me."

"I do love you," he shot back. "But—"

She cut him off. "Don't you dare say you're

doing this for me, Jacob Holt," she snapped. "Don't hide behind that lie." She began to cry, but these weren't weepy tears of sadness. These were mad streaks of water that seemed to cut into her face. "And here I thought you wanted me—you wanted our *family*. I can't count on you, can I?"

"What are you going to do—have me investigated?" he said. Okay, shouted. "Try to dig up more information you can take back to your father so you can be Daddy's little girl again?"

"Go to hell." She opened the door and got out.

"Skye—wait!" He yelled after her, scrambling to get out of the car. She didn't turn around. An old panic flooded his system. Once, he'd lost her because he hadn't fought for her. That's not how he was going to go down this time. There'd be no words left unspoken, not this time. "Skye, dammit—wait. I'm not going to take the job. I don't even know why we're arguing over it. Things have changed. I've changed. Remember?" He tried to get in front of her, to make her listen, but she was pretty darned fast for a woman in her condition.

Before he could stop her, she wrenched Keaton's front door open and stepped inside. "I don't want to hear it." She turned and gave him a look full of heartache and pain. "You didn't even *tell* me about the interview. You lied to me, Jake. What is it about this damn job—this damn company of yours—that means more to you than I do? Than our baby does?"

"It doesn't," he insisted, closing the distance between them.

"This is why I wanted a divorce, isn't it? This is *exactly* why. We got a second chance and what did you do? You made me think you'd changed. But you haven't. *You haven't*. And it's clear you won't change for me. Not now, not ever."

She slammed the door shut in his face. The lock clicked.

Hell. He rang the doorbell, but no one answered; all he heard was that dog howling. He had no choice here. He grabbed his phone and called Keaton.

"Damn your hide," he snarled when his brother picked up. "Why did you tell Skye about that interview? I'm not even going to take the job!"

In the stunned silence that followed, he was pretty sure he heard crying in the background. God, it just went from bad to worse.

"Damn—Jake, I didn't mean to set her off."

"You never mean it, do you?" He couldn't even talk to his brother. Jake hung up. He was done with that man. *Done* with him. This was why Jake didn't want to come back to Royal—his family would always fail him when he needed them most.

Part of him wanted to go after Skye, try to talk some sense into her. But another part of him knew that would be a bad idea. She was already upset. He wanted her to calm down first. Which left only one thing to do.

Jake punched up Lark's number. "Skye's upset," he began when she answered the phone. "She doesn't want to stay with me right now. She's in your house with Keaton."

Lark gasped. "What happened?"

"She's remembering," Jake said. He knew that Skye would probably tell Lark everything, but he couldn't bear to throw himself under that bus. "I've got to try and fix this, but if you could keep a close eye on her until she calms down…"

"Of course. My shift is almost over, anyway. I can be home in twenty minutes."

"Thanks, Lark. I owe you." He hung up again and stared at his damn phone.

Had he changed? He wanted to think he had.

He was a father now, after all. That alone changed a man.

But…

He jammed his hands into his pockets, trying to think. What was it about this damn company? That's what she wanted to know. Why did it mean so much to him?

Because it was his. He'd started it on his own, with no help from his family. He'd been free of them.

Except he hadn't been, not really. Everything he'd done had been a reaction to them, to the way they'd tried to keep him from Skye.

Something poked him in the finger. He pulled out the small baggie with an earring and a half in it. A single diamond was all that was left of the jewelry he'd bought for Skye.

He knew what he had to do. He wasn't going to like this, but it had to be done.

He got in the car and headed toward the Taylor place.

# Thirteen

"What are *you* doing here?" was how Tyrone Taylor answered the door.

"I need to talk to you." When the older man didn't move, Jake added, "It's about Skye and Grace."

Tyrone didn't give much—but he gave enough. His eyebrows shot up in barely concealed concern and he didn't slam the door in Jake's face.

The man was a tyrant and a bully, but Jake had to hope that maybe—just maybe—he could convince him to make the right call on behalf of his daughter. Jake wasn't even going to attempt to sway Vera Taylor. Tyrone was his target.

"Are they—are they okay?" Tyrone's voice sounded soft, which was unusual enough.

"Doing good," Jake said. No need to torture the older man. "That's not why I'm here, though. There are some things you need to know. I married your daughter four years ago. And you know what? The one thing she wanted was the one thing I didn't want to give her—that was you. She wanted you to walk her down the aisle. She wanted to know that you and Vera still loved her. And I didn't think you two deserved to know how much she still loved you."

That—that was the heart of the matter. Their families didn't deserve them because they'd always put the damned feud before Jake and Skye.

Which was what Jake had done with his job and Skye.

Well, no more. Those days were over.

Tyrone's face reddened, but again, he didn't slam the door. "She made her choice. You."

"Don't you even want to know your grandchildren?" That was the only leverage that Jake had and both men knew it.

"Now, you listen here, Jake Holt—"

"No, I'm done listening to you." He thrust the

copy of the land deed filed in the state office a hundred and fourteen years ago. "A Taylor moved the fences. You've been on Holt land your entire life."

"Your brother forged that document," Tyrone sputtered. "He didn't find it at town hall. He made it up."

"Even if that were true, how do you explain this one? Skye hired a private detective who found this in the Texas General Land Office. They have the original on file."

"Lies," Tyrone spat. "Another fake."

"The original has been rediscovered," Jake said. "On file. For anyone—and their lawyers—to see it." Tyrone almost dropped the folder, as if the reality had burned him. "Here's the deal, Taylor. I'm going to move back here with Skye. Keaton's going to marry Lark. The land will stay in both of our families. You can either dig in your blowhard heels and never see your granddaughter ever again or you can suck it up, admit that your ancestor was a thief and do what's best for your family."

The older man's mouth opened, shut, opened and shut again.

*And the truth shall set you free*, Jake thought. "I want to make Skye happy. I want to give her the one thing I could never give her before—her family. Even if you and your wife don't deserve it, Skye loves both of you and she wants our daughter to know you both."

Tyrone's mouth continued to open and shut as he turned from a tomato red to an eggplant purple.

"I'm going to throw a little party for her," Jake went on. "A reengagement party."

He could get the diamond from her earring set into a ring mount in a day or two—sooner, if the price was right.

This was what he had to do to show her that she meant more than the job. He had to marry her all over again—this time, with both of their families' approval. "I'd appreciate it if you and *Vera*," he went on, struggling to get the name out without scowling, "could come and be happy for our family. For *your* family."

Tyrone looked at the folder, then at Jake.

Yeah, they were done here. Jake didn't think he could pin the old man down to a yes, not when he'd put Tyrone on the spot. So he just said, "Friday night, at the Holt ranch, if you decide to come." Then he turned and went home.

He had a marriage proposal to arrange.

* * *

At several points, Skye found herself on the verge of asking Lark if Jake had said anything to her. Lark's phone was certainly ringing a lot. Plus, when Lark answered it, she'd shoot Skye a nervous smile and immediately leave the room. Something was clearly up.

But the moment Skye would start to find the words, Lark would suddenly notice something *very interesting* that Grace was doing that Lark had to just gush over.

Had Jake taken the job? Had he picked the company over her again?

It was almost too much to bear. Because if the answer was yes, what was she going to do?

Divorce him? She didn't remember what she'd been thinking when she'd filed the first time. Had she hoped that the papers would be a wake-up call? Or had she been completely serious about it? It didn't even appear that she'd told him about her pregnancy. Maybe she had been serious.

She didn't know. What was worse, she didn't know when she'd know—or if she ever would. Those ten months were nearly blank and there was no one who'd been around to fill in the blanks for her.

Did she want a divorce?

She thought about how Jake had been the one to take her home from the hospital, to take care of her even when he knew she'd filed for divorce.

She knew now that all of that was radically different from how he'd been for a while—maybe as long as a year, even. And the things he'd said to her, while he was waiting for her to remember?

*Whatever happened in the past isn't as important as what happens in the future, Skye.*

Maybe…maybe she was asking for too much. He'd poured his heart and soul into his company. Obviously, the work made him happy. Who was she to ask him to give that up?

She was his wife. The mother of his child.

God, she just didn't know what to do.

Jake kept calling, talking to Keaton or Lark. They always asked if she'd like to talk to him, but she didn't know what to say. He'd asked questions—good ones—about whether she'd been planning on giving the deed to her father or to his family. And she just didn't have an answer for him. She might never have one.

Lark tried to keep her occupied with Grace. Skye didn't see much of Keaton, but she figured he was probably steering clear of her. It wasn't as lonely as it had been when Jake had left her the last time—she had Lark and Grace—but it was uncomfortably close.

Then Gloria came over Friday afternoon. Skye was so happy to see the older woman that she started to cry again. "Oh, now," Gloria said as she wrapped Skye up in a motherly hug. "Everyone fights, dear. It's not the fight that matters so much as how you make up."

"But *how*? I don't know what I don't know. Oh, God," she sobbed onto Gloria's shoulder.

Gloria sighed. "Jake and my David got on like oil and water, but they're more alike than either of them realize—both set in their ways and too stubborn for their own good. But," she went on, striking a hopeful note, "they just need a little space to regroup."

"Have you talked to him?" Skye demanded tearfully.

"I have," Gloria said. "Don't give up on him, Skye. He hasn't given up on you. Now," she added in a more forceful tone before Skye could question her further, "sitting around moping isn't going to help anything. I think we should have a little outing, don't you? It's warmer today. We could bundle Grace up and go out to the ranch. Won't that be fun?" Then she got up and bustled out of the room, describing all the ways that such an outing would be "fun."

Which was a crock, as far as Skye was concerned. Something was up.

"What's going on?" Skye demanded when Lark and Gloria came back into the room.

"Nothing!" both women said at the same time. There was no missing the look the two of them shared.

"I've got Grace," Gloria said with a smug smile. "You two girls go on."

"What's going on?" Skye demanded again as Lark led her to the bedroom and pointed out a bright blue sweater that Lark had apparently picked out on her own. "I mean, this is lovely, but seriously? The last time you brought me clothing, I had a baby shower."

"Sit," Lark commanded, leading Skye into the bathroom and pointedly avoiding the question.

"I've almost figured out how to use a curling iron. This will be nice!"

"The more you and Gloria say that, the less I believe you," Skye mumbled. "Easy on the sore spot!"

Lark ignored her complaints. Instead, she said, "Can I tell you something?" as she wielded the curling iron like it was a weapon.

"Always," Skye said, resigning herself to her lot in life.

"I'm pregnant."

Skye sat up so fast she almost caught her forehead on the curling iron. "You are? Oh, Lark!"

Lark grinned, the happiness radiating off of her. "And Keaton and I already discussed it—if it's a girl, we're going to name her Taylor."

"Taylor Holt? I *love* it." It was a perfect name— the two families finally reunited.

"You do?" Lark beamed. "I'm not that far along, so we aren't going to tell everyone yet, but I wanted you to know."

"Oh, Lark," Skye said, her eyes starting to fill with tears. She managed to get to her feet without hitting the hot iron and wrapped her sister in a big hug. "I want our children to grow up together."

"I know. I want things to be better than it was for us, you know?" She leaned back and fanned her eyes. "Sorry. I'm already getting more emotional."

"Don't apologize. Have you and Keaton talked about getting married any more?"

Lark grinned as she went back to curling Skye's hair. She kept up a steady patter—she and Keaton wanted to get married this summer, before Lark started to show. Then maybe they'd take a honeymoon cruise to Alaska. "Or something, as long as we're together," Lark said as she blushed.

Finally, the torture with the curling iron was done. After Lark had misted her hair with spray, saying, "Even Mom would be proud of *that*," she then insisted that Skye let her put on a little blush and some mascara. "You'll feel better with a little makeup on," Lark added, with that sneaky smile that Skye hadn't trusted for decades.

Skye sighed. Clearly something was up. But she didn't know what.

Finally, Lark's phone buzzed. She looked at the

message, pronounced Skye "beautiful" and not-so-casually said, "We should go."

"There's a party downstairs, isn't there?" Skye said.

"Of course not," Lark said way too fast.

"Is there any way out of this? I'm not feeling social right now. I just want Jake."

"Trust me," Lark replied with that smile again.

Lark and Gloria got Grace all bundled up in her baby carrier so wind couldn't get to her. Then everyone was in the car. Skye decided to sit in the back so she could keep an eye on her daughter.

She didn't want to go out to the ranch house. She didn't want people to try to cheer her up.

She just wanted Jake. She wanted things to go back to the way they were.

Well, not really. She wanted the closeness they used to have, back when they'd first run off, but she wanted to spend time with her sister and Gloria and maybe, one day, her own parents. She wanted Grace to grow up with her cousins, to know her aunt and uncle and grandparents. She wanted the community where near strangers would throw her a baby shower and be happy for her recovery.

She wanted it all. And she wanted Jake to want that, too.

The drive out to the Holt homestead was not quiet. Gloria could keep up quite a conversation all by herself, but Lark was right there with her. Skye figured they weren't leaving a silent moment, lest she start asking questions again.

So she sat in the backseat and watched Grace sleep underneath her blankets and half listened as Gloria talked about the lovely retirement community they were looking at in Gulf Shores.

Finally, they pulled up at the ranch house. Skye looked around, but she didn't see any signs of a party. No cars parked everywhere, no people milling about. Good. She didn't want to celebrate anything, anyway.

Lark unfastened Grace's carrier and Gloria said, "I'll help you get her inside. Skye, why don't you just sit tight for a moment?"

She looked at them. "No, that's not suspicious at all."

But the two women just laughed and headed inside.

Skye managed to get out of the car. She stood there, holding on to the door for support, and looked around. Oh, she'd missed these wide-open spaces. Even though the wind was blowing and the grass was brown and dry, this feeling of freedom was something she just couldn't get in Houston.

Houston. All of her things were still there. Heck, as far as she knew, her wedding ring was still on the ground outside their apartment. She would have to find a way to go there and…

Stay? Pack up and come back here?

Would Jake be there for any of that? Or would she be on her own?

She heard the front door shut and turned, expecting to see Lark coming back for her. Except it wasn't Lark.

It was Jake.

"Where have you been?" was the first thing out of her mouth. She immediately winced at how bitchy it sounded.

"Working," he said as he came around the car.

"Oh. Of course." She turned her face back to the land. She didn't want to stay in Houston. This was where Grace belonged. And since Jake obviously wasn't going to be a part of the future…

She didn't get too far along that path because suddenly, Jake was in front of her and he was folding her into his arms and holding her against his chest and she let him, damn it. She let him because she didn't know if she'd ever get to hold him like this again.

"Skye," he said.

She was not going to cry at the goodbye. "Yes?" She was going to *try* not to cry, anyway.

"I didn't take the job."

"You *what*?" She jolted back and stared up at him.

"I didn't take it. I told you I wasn't going to," he added with a small smile. "I realized that you were right. The job—the company—will never love me back. It'll keep taking and taking until I don't have anything left to give and all it'll ever give me back is money. And money can't love me. Not like you do, Skye."

"Oh, Jake," she said as tears began to slip free. "I've never stopped loving you. Not even when you drive me nuts."

He laughed at this and kissed her cheeks where

the tears had left a trail. "I didn't tell you about the interview because I hadn't decided if I wanted the job or not and I didn't want to upset you. I guess…I was trying to have things both ways and it didn't work. I'm sorry for that. I've decided to take a step back from doing the jobs myself. I'm going to start hiring guys to be on-site so I can stay here with you. It's a little like promoting myself to management," he added with a grin.

"You're going to stay? With me?" She gasped, unsure if she was dreaming or if this was really real.

"You're the one I want, the one person on this earth I need more than anything else." He stroked her cheeks with his thumbs. "I can't walk away from you, Skye. I never could."

"I shouldn't have gotten upset," she admitted. "It's just that everything feels so new in my head—like a year ago is happening at the same time as right now and I'm not sure I'm doing the best job of keeping the past separate from the future. I know you have to work."

"Don't apologize, Skye," he told her as he held her against his chest.

"But I threw away your ring and filed for

divorce and I can't remember if I wanted a divorce or if I just wanted to force you to choose. I didn't try hard enough, Jake. And I want to try harder."

"Babe," he said and then he kissed her, hot and hard, and it was everything she wanted from him.

When the kiss ended, he said, "I have something else to apologize for." But he didn't sound sad about it.

"What?" she asked, almost afraid to hear the answer.

"Come inside," he said in a gentle voice. "I have something I want to show you."

She didn't want to. She wanted to stay out here with him where they could get everything settled—the right way, this time. But he'd asked. And she was showing him that she put their relationship first. "All right."

Smiling, Jake escorted her inside. The moment she stepped into the hall, she heard the low hum that went with a bunch of people trying to all whisper at the same time. "Jake?" she asked.

"It turns out," he said, "that I wanted to do something to show you that our relationship was more important to me than anything else, too."

They turned the corner and walked down into

the living room. Easily thirty people were standing around, drinks in hand.

Gloria and David Holt were up front, standing next to Lark and Keaton. Grace was in David's arms, and he looked as happy as Skye had ever seen him. And next to them…

"Dad? Mom?" Skye gasped. Her parents were there, looking only moderately uncomfortable.

"There's my girl," Tyrone Taylor said.

"If I could have your attention," Jake said. Then he got down on one knee and there was a ring in his hand. "Will you marry me all over again, Skye? This is the only diamond they could find after the tornado. We can't go back where we were before, but we can make our love new again."

Skye stared down at the diamond—familiar, yet not. She was so stunned that she couldn't even answer. She looked around, feeling overwhelmed.

Her father stepped forward. "I'd like to walk you down the aisle, Skye. That is, if you still want me to. The Taylors and Holts," he said, managing not to sneer in the direction of Gloria and David, "well, we have more in common than I'd given us credit for. We can find a way to coexist. For the sake of the grandchildren."

Vera Taylor sniffed, but for once in her life, she said nothing.

"That's true enough," David said, not looking at Tyrone.

"And we hope you two decide to stay here in Royal," Gloria added before anyone could start sniping.

"Yes," Lark said. Keaton stood behind her, his arms around her waist. "Stay."

Jake turned to her. His hand reached for hers and he smiled hopefully at her. "It's what you wanted, right?"

"Oh, Jake," Skye said. She wanted to say more—how much she loved him, how much she'd dreamed of this moment—but she didn't have any words left.

So she did the only thing she could to show him how she felt.

She kissed him. Hard.

And as everyone cheered at this yes, Jake kissed her back. "I lost you once. It won't ever happen again, I promise you that," he said in a low voice meant only for her ears. "Let me prove it to you every single day for the rest of our lives."

Skye held him to her, unafraid of what her parents or his parents might say. She could hear people talking—sounds of approval flowed around her. But there was no one but Jake. There never had been and there never would be. "I love you, Jake Holt."

He slid the ring onto her finger. It felt different from the other ring—heavier—but she was different now, too. And different could be better.

"I love you too, my blue-eyed Skye."

Then they went to greet their family.

Together.

\* \* \* \* \*

# MILLS & BOON®

## Why shop at millsandboon.co.uk?

Each year, thousands of romance readers find their perfect read at millsandboon.co.uk. That's because we're passionate about bringing you the very best romantic fiction. Here are some of the advantages of shopping at www.millsandboon.co.uk:

* **Get new books first**—you'll be able to buy your favourite books one month before they hit the shops

* **Get exclusive discounts**—you'll also be able to buy our specially created monthly collections, with up to 50% off the RRP

* **Find your favourite authors**—latest news, interviews  and new releases for all your favourite authors and series on our website, plus ideas for what to try next

* **Join in**—once you've bought your favourite books, don't forget to register with us to rate, review and join in the discussions

Visit **www.millsandboon.co.uk**
for all this and more today!